e-mail from a jewish mother

MONA BERMAN

david philip publishers
cape town

First published in 2001 by David Philip Publishers
an imprint of New Africa Books (Pty) Ltd,
99 Garfield Road, Kenilworth, 7700, South Africa

Second impression 2002

ISBN 0-86486-372-1

Printed and bound in South Africa by Clyson Printers,
Maitland, Cape Town

D8717

Acknowledgements

My thanks to Orenna, Judie and Marie, my first readers; to Sheila, who made me rewrite the manuscript, with more than words; and to Lisa, whose insightful editing brought the book to closure.

This is a work of fiction based on my world. Where the events and characters are too close to the bone it is because I was unable to invent any person or situation that amused me more.

As for my daughters – women who run with the wolves – they are in the pages of the book only where I have managed to tame a small part of them.

For Lionel, who believed in my book,
who gave me the courage to complete it and who helped
make the process of writing it such fun

31 January

My dear Sarah

Why do you say e-mail is meant for short messages and not long letters? I telephoned a number of computer companies to ask whether long letters by e-mail are OK and they all told me it's fine. So, obviously you have been wrongly informed, or living in England is finally getting to you. And don't say I didn't warn you. The Brits are a cold, unfeeling people and know nothing about a mother's need to feel close to her children. I must admit that Leah said something similar to me about long e-mails, so I suppose the same can be said about the awful Aussies! I realise that I am sending my letters to you at work, but until that husband of yours decides to get a nice Apple Mac for you at home and earns enough money for you not to have to go out to work, I have no choice. Tell him what I said. On second thought you had better not. I don't want to make trouble between the two of you. Mind you, I think he needs to be told a thing or two.

In fact, I intend writing Cedric a nice letter to thank him for letting me sleep next to you in your double bed for my two-week stay in London. I'm sure he could not have been too comfortable on the floor in the living room/dining room/foyer/kitchen or whatever you call the downstairs of your quaint little house. But, as he explained to me, he was closer to the television and was accustomed to your two cats jumping all over him in the middle of the night. And he was not as likely to catch cold as I was from the chilly air blowing through the cracks in the walls, doors and window frames. His spine, I'm sure, is more resilient than mine – the better to cope with sleeping on the floor. And it would have been quite stifling for me in the sleeping bag with my hot flushes and everything else I have to endure on my visits to my children. As a child I never went camping and therefore I have no experience of the rough-and-ready lifestyle. But, I must say, the king-size bed is extremely comfortable and, but for the guilt feelings waking me up every hour, I would really have enjoyed the excellent orthopaedic mattress. The bed, of course, is the only major piece of furniture you have in your two and a half rooms, and I'm not saying this because I bought it for you. I want you to know that it is a better bed than the one I have at home.

I wonder what it is with that husband of yours. Even though he is not Jewish, he is a clever boy and has very nice manners, but where does he get his crazy ideas from? I know that he is an inventor and designer, but can't he behave like other people? Why does he need to build steel shelves in the living room/dining room/foyer/kitchen for his French steel-bottom pots and pans? Is it to match that fancy designer stove he bought or that fridge that looks like a steel sculpture? Isn't it more important for you to have chairs to sit on – not those awkward Indian cushions for meditation that only the cats seem to enjoy? I tried to show him that I was impressed with the copper piping for the hot water, and the ingenious electricity cupboard that does away with unseemly wires on skirting boards – if you had any – but does it really matter? Am I supposed to tell my friends that my daughter is living in a council house with no furniture but with a wonderful electrical system, steel switch covers and dimmer light switches?

I am also going to compliment Cedric on his cooking. He seems to have the knack of knowing just how long to cook pasta. I must admit that when I cook pasta it's either undercooked or over-cooked, but it hardly matters because I don't eat much pasta except when I'm in Italy. I know that sometimes you have it with a tomato type sauce, sometimes with basil or broccoli, but how can you face it every night, even though you are a vegetarian? I know it's cheap and easy to cook if you know how, but could you not vary your diet a bit? I didn't mind for myself, because I knew it was just for two weeks, but I kept thinking about the variety of wholesome Jewish dishes you used to enjoy at home. As far as I was concerned, I became quite philosophical about the menu. Linguini is filling and healthier than takeaway food favoured by many young working couples.

I also intend telling Cedric that I think he is a very good father to my darling Seja. An unlikely father but very solicitous. I think he really plays his part in fetching her from the nursery school when you come home late in the evening after your commute on the tube, bus and train. I know he has to deal with the traffic from his place of work as well, but he is after all sitting in a comfortable car with nice taped music and amusing distractions en route. I am also impressed by his taking Seja to the crèche on occasion in the mornings when you have early meetings and have to leave before seven a.m. while it's still dark in that dreary climate.

I agree that Cedric should limit the amount of television your four-year-old sees, but how do you explain to her that it's OK for Daddy to watch Formula1 racing for three hours at a stretch yet it's not good for her to watch Teletubbies for twenty minutes? It's a real problem to explain that kind of logic to a four-year-old. She can't grasp a basic concept like the beneficial aspect of viewing

3

sport on television, lessening stress while providing necessary relaxation from daily pressures at work. It is one of the big challenges facing parents in rearing children: how to set them a good example not by what you do but by what you say.

Since my visit with you I have had many sleepless nights. I cannot understand the relevance of your depressing job with the British Labour Ministry trying to sort out problems of the globalisation of the poor. I keep wondering why you have chosen to live on the breadline in England instead of reaping the benefits of our new democracy. It hardly helped my state of mind when I bumped into your old varsity friend Zanaida Rasool while shopping in Rosebank. She looks marvellous – very chic – and is as friendly and delightful as ever. She wanted to know all about you and so we decided to abandon our shopping chores and went to Dino's, your favourite coffee bar, where we gossiped for almost two hours.

Zanaida has this brilliant job with the Constitutional Court, and it seems that her legal background and experience in fighting human rights cases has been invaluable for the kind of work she is doing. She told me about several of your mutual friends who also have great jobs in government: Frank in the Department of Arts and Culture, Sipho in land distribution, Alex in the driver's seat of Water Affairs in the North West Province. Unfortunately, Mpho Nibanda has been axed from her portfolio in Housing and Development, and Nat Nkomo, who was such a brilliant medical student, has bungled a top job in the Department of Health. But on the whole, most of your friends and colleagues are doing exceptionally well. Some have moved into the corporate world, while others have prominent positions of power in government. They all live in nice big homes and drive the latest Mercedes Benz or BMW. Their children are in excellent private schools and they are now enjoying their lives in comfort, working towards a renaissance in the country of their birth.

Sarah, I must tell you in all honesty that I was quite embarrassed to explain your circumstances to Zanaida. I mean, you and Cedric sacrificed the best years of your youth to the struggle for democracy in our country, and now that we have it you are struggling to make ends meet in an alien land. Is there any good reason for you not to be living here among the people for whom you care so much? Do you think that there is something noble about being poor and not having the things you need – and that you are going to be rewarded for your honesty, your moral courage and principles? I cannot understand why you are living in a dreary council house with the dullest neighbours, an hour out of London, trying to earn enough so that your child can be educated in a bloody British stiff-upper-lip democracy.

Come home, Sarah! Most South African Jewish mothers want their children to get out of the country, but I want mine to come home where they belong. Africa is in your blood, but you know that better than I do. I know the crime rate is appalling, but we are certainly not the crime capital of the world as the British media suggests. We need people like you to help fight it, not run away from it. We have much more cultural diversity in our own backyard than in all of England. We have every shade of colour, every religious denomination, every class of people from scumbags to saints in our society. You only have to walk the streets to see that Johannesburg is the new melting pot of the world. Why has your positive optimistic outlook disappeared? It was something which you taught us all in those dark years of apartheid and which kept you going. I encouraged you both to complete your studies in England and gain experience in the workplace. But now that you are qualified to make a significant difference to the transformation process, you have become like other expatriates, frightened of a future in South Africa.

I live in hope.

Much love
Mom

6 February

My dearest Leah

Is it really true that you now have your own computer and e-mail address? How relieved I am that I no longer have to write to you via your husband's computer. Don't misunderstand me. You know very well how I adore Sam and value him as a son-in-law, but I have never felt comfortable in sharing personal correspondence either with him or with my wonderful grandchildren. It is not that I am suggesting that you should have secrets from one another, but conversations between mothers and daughters are private.

I have almost become immune to Sam's mother-in-law jokes and the stories he always repeats to your children and friends which never fail to amuse him, particularly the ones he embellishes – how he pushed me into the swimming pool fully clothed, or tripped me down the mountain on a hiking trip or left me stranded in the middle of a river while we were water-skiing. Of course I don't believe there is anything sinister in his practical jokes, in spite of what he tells his friends. He simply loves to tease me. So you can understand why I would prefer that he does not read my e-mail to you. The same goes for the children, especially the oldest ones, who seem to be computer whiz-kids. Can you imagine them showing my correspondence to their classmates? I might as well publish it in a book for the world to see.

About Gavriela's Batmitzvah celebration: I agree that it provides the perfect opportunity for Sarah and Rebecca and their families to come to Australia for a grand reunion, and I share your elation. In all the years you have been in Perth, they have not been able to visit you, for financial and other reasons. After all, it is not as though Australia is on the way to anywhere, nor have I heard that travel agents offer cheap rates to down under, so it is hardly surprising that we have never yet managed to fulfil your dream of a momentous get-together in your adopted city. It is disappointing that Rachel cannot be there because of the imminent baby.

What a splendid idea to have a dinner dance in a hall with caterers. The relief I feel is immense. I was feeling exhausted just thinking about feeding those hundreds of guests, setting tables, arranging flowers and doing all those other countless chores needed to make a success of any *simcha*. I can recall every single celebration we have catered for – birthdays, brisses, baby-naming parties, those *opsherinis* celebrations where your poor three-year-old sons were traumatised when everyone took a turn at cutting their hair, the Pesach meals, the Rosh Hashanah celebrations, the meals for seven days in the *succah*, the baking of Shavuot cheese blintzes and Purim *homentassen*, the Chanukkah excitement each evening as the candles are lit, the festivals re-enacted each year. And now finally you have agreed to delegate someone else to do the hard work for the Batmitzvah and allow the family to behave like real guests. What more can a mother ask for?

Of course, I will still bring my chopped herring and *kichel* that you enjoy so much, but not the usual quantity to feed hordes – just enough for the Friday night Shabbat dinner. That way I can still manage to bring some *taiglach* in ginger syrup that Sam loves so much. Mind you, it is a real problem bringing food into

8

Australia, what with their ridiculous laws and the sniffer dogs that always find the carefully wrapped and disguised food. It was so embarrassing for me on my last visit when I was discovered smuggling kosher biltong in my luggage. Not only did they confiscate it but I had to pay a hefty fine – with the price of biltong these days it was an extravagance I could ill afford. I was lucky that the customs official was sympathetic to my story of deprived grandchildren, otherwise I might have been detained! I am indebted to my friend Gertie, who travels to visit her children in Perth all the time and knows how to freeze and vacuum-pack herring, *tzimmes* and all delicatessen without being found out. She assures me it is perfectly legal as long as the food is cooked and sealed.

While I don't want to pay overweight charges on my luggage, if there is something special that the children want me to make, like my almond biscuits, I will do so.

I intend to start baking, cooking and freezing very soon.

Much love
Mom

26 February

Rachel my dearest

I really loved spending the week with you. Durban can be really nice sometimes and I'm grateful that you are living only seven hundred kilometres away. Small mercies! The journey home was pretty good except for those wild taxi drivers in their bashed-in tin combis weaving in and out of the traffic. I was also careful to keep clear of the speeding buses that suddenly appear from nowhere and aggressively overtake you on the bends. They look as though they are ready for the scrapyard.

I have been worried sick about you since I'm home. I'm deeply concerned about your work situation, particularly as you are about to have a baby. Let me state clearly, so you don't get the wrong idea, that I am enormously proud of the work you do and I think your profession as a play therapist is perfectly fine, even though no one seems to know what it actually is. I don't even mind that people are generally ignorant about alternative therapy, because I believe that one day it will be recognised as a really useful profession.

Your contribution to the community at large is commendable, although I don't understand why you choose such depressing people to work with and why you go to such dangerous places to do your work. With your brains and talent you could be living in a more upmarket suburb, attracting wealthy clients to an elegant studio and building up a lucrative practice. Instead, you have chosen to do most of your outreach work in ramshackle buildings that are falling apart, while your private paying clients are being treated in your eccentrically furnished garden studio where, you assure me, they feel at ease and comfortable with their surroundings. I am not suggesting a hostile or elitist environment, but would it hurt if your consulting room looked pleasant and was tastefully furnished and decent?

I need some answers from you. Why when you are five months pregnant do you choose to rush off to the townships, visit the schools that can't afford to pay you, become involved in prisons and courtrooms for abused children and work in that dreadful centre for violence, rape and abuse? What did I do to deserve this? All my friends' children have nice jobs in nice places if they have to work. I admit that not many have real jobs, most helping their husbands who are doctors, lawyers or businessmen in their practices with reception work or bookkeeping. Well, I don't blame you for not wanting to do office work, nor am I complaining that your husband isn't a doctor or lawyer or a director of companies. Though if he were, I admit that I would sleep better at night.

It is so degrading and demeaning for you to be canvassing for funding of all your projects. You might as well wear a placard and join the street beggars. Surely the government should give you money to what you do for the poor and disadvantaged. Why do you have to go to schools in the townships to train teachers who are already trained or run workshops in courtrooms in unsafe areas to conscientise magistrates about their onerous task when dealing with women and children who have been raped and abused? I realise that there has to be change in their attitudes and in the judicial process, and I know that someone needs to do it, but why you? I'm sure they find it difficult to deal with a little slip of a pale pregnant girl advising them as to their obligation to protect the victims from the perpetrators who are so indiscriminately let loose again. I know we have a new constitution, I know that we as women have to uphold and fight for basic human rights, and I know that by choosing to live in this country we can no longer pretend to ignore injustice and inequity. I am not saying that I don't sympathise with your 'do-good' attitude, but I think your energies should be focused on more pleasant things and less stressful matters.

Rachel dear, I know you will tell me to stop living in a dream world where things are as we would wish them to be. I am aware that it is increasingly difficult to live without stress in our society, where violence and rape are daily occurrences and where the escalation of domestic violence is symptomatic of a society under siege. I agree that violent crime is more intense and present here than in most other places and therefore the transformational process, while a wonderfully liberating necessity, has its own agenda of seemingly insurmountable difficulties. But do you have to be one of the pioneers in this field? Your responsibility is to your husband, your child, your unborn child and to your mother who brought you into this world in the first place.

Although I consider you fairly well adjusted and able to cope with your work, family and home, I cannot help wondering where I went wrong with your upbringing. Some of my friends, and I'm thinking particularly of Nora and Mercia, who over-indulged their daughters produced nice normal kugels with nice normal ambitions. What is wrong with staying at home with your child, having your friends over for tea, enjoying married life? Instead, you are always tired and worn out and you never seem to be able to afford to go to nice places and to buy nice clothes. I tried to give you the best of everything and now those things are no longer important to you. Where are your values? You're always focusing on others with no time or money for yourself. You're forever rushing around doing workshop and group therapy sessions, raising funds for your projects, training teachers and educators – whereas it is you who needs to be retrained to enjoy a decent lifestyle.

I'm sure if you were living in Johannesburg your quality of life would be much better. At least I would be around to help you on a day-to-day basis. Why can't Eli be transferred back here?

Please try and take greater care of yourself.

Much love
Mom

2 March

Rachel my dearest

I am having recurring nightmares picturing you in labour while
painting murals in one of the prison courtrooms in Umlazi.
Imagine giving birth in that dirty dreary courtroom assisted by
untrained magistrates or policemen with an audience of sexual
offenders! Horrors! I know you have told me that I must not
become paranoid about things that may not happen, or imagine
the unimaginable. But the notion of my grandchild being born in
a courtroom drama is more than a mother can bear!

I was so pleased when you married Eli because I thought he
would be the perfect husband to keep you on track. He is so level-
headed, has such a pleasant disposition and is so practically mind-
ed. I am proud of his professional expertise as an electronics and
technical engineer who can fix anything. But now, after my visit to
you, I have discovered that he considers himself a master builder
as well. I find it most disturbing the way he is continually building
on to your house, knocking out walls, putting in wooden windows
and doors, making alterations and extensions to the bathroom
and kitchen, changing every wall and ceiling. It seems to me that
his behaviour has become compulsive and addictive. I'm also
wondering whether you have caused it. This continuing desire to
build on to your house, even after there is no longer any space,

has forced him to go underground. When I mentioned this to Roger, my next-door neighbour, who is a well-regarded building contractor, he was horrified. He told me quite categorically, 'Burrowing under the foundations of a house to build a basement office and playroom seriously undermines its structure.' He did not mention the exorbitant cost of the building exercise and I keep wondering whether you can afford this extra expense. But Eli assures me that his technical diploma in plumbing has given him sufficient expertise to make structural changes to your house and that the cost will be minimal. He laughed at my suggestion to call in a structural engineer for advice, and I had the distinct impression that he thought I was interfering in matters I know nothing about.

I am the first to admit that when Eli was courting you, one of the attractions for me was his trade as a plumber. As you know, I always had this fantasy that if I had a son, he would be a plumber. My aspirations were not for my daughters to marry professionals – the doctor/lawyer/accountant kick that all my friends favoured never impressed me much. I found the notion of 'my son, the plumber' much more appealing – and my thinking was not influenced by the financial rewards of such a profession. But, alas, he needed loftier challenges in his life. I mean, he married you.

I can't pretend I was not disappointed when he changed careers to become an electronics engineer for one of those big corporations, particularly as they transferred him to their head office in Durban. It now appears that he is the only person left in the country who can install and fix electronically advanced computer-driven machinery. Now they are sending him all over the country to install and maintain their monstrous machines. I mean, why did you have to move from Johannesburg if he is forever travelling?

It just doesn't make sense to me – he now has joined the rat race and increased his stress levels, and is spending less time with his family. He is so busy that even when he comes to visit me I feel embarrassed to ask him to fix the simplest leak in my toilet, adjust my watering system or mend a broken pipe. I am intimidated by his expertise and cannot bring myself to ask him to change the fuse on my electrical board, let alone dare ask him to programme a basic function key on my computer that would save me hours of 'copy and paste'. He always has so many more important things to do!

Why is it that I am the last person who is consulted when my children change direction and rush into a field that is uncharted?

Much love
Mom

4 March

Rachel dearest

Thanks for your quick reply. I wish you wouldn't always take things out of context and become so defensive.

I suppose you are right that it is unfair of me to criticise Eli's opportunity for advancement in a corporate environment just because I always enjoyed telling my friends about my son, the plumber – that he is the salt of the earth, performing an essential service and engaged in a universal trade that requires both technical skill and manual labour. But, being married to a therapist and with his growing family commitments, he would, I suppose, inevitably have to change to a more fashionable career with executive prospects.

As for your criticism of me changing directions without consulting my children or friends, I suppose you are right again. No, I did not ask advice when I decided to change my life and get divorced from your father after thirty-plenty years of marriage. At least I didn't inconvenience any of you – I waited until you were all nicely settled before I took the leap. At one stage I did consider asking your advice, but I felt it was unfair. It would have meant that you would have had to take sides. I hated the idea of any of my children acting as marriage counsellors. In the past your father and I had patched up our relationship so many times that it seemed pointless to keep repeating that procedure. I also thought that none of you would believe me when I said that finally I had had enough, that I wanted out. I had cried wolf many times before, but somehow your father and I had always managed to pick up the pieces and resume our lifestyle. I was also afraid that someone would stop me this time – tell me how ridiculous I was being, how impractical and impossible divorce was going to be for me after being married my entire post-teen life. And so I took a decision, the most difficult one of my life, but I believe it was *bershert* – meant to be.

But at no stage did I foresee that one of the consequences of the divorce was losing all my friends at the same time. I was so anxious about my children's reaction that I never imagined it would cause such an upheaval in our social circle. It was as though I had betrayed our mutual friends. I had committed the unpardonable act of rocking the boat – making waves in apparently calm waters. The reaction of my friends and acquaintances to my divorce was bizarre. It was as though the Northern Suburban Clan called an emergency meeting and declared me a traitor, an enemy of the status quo. Husbands warned wives not to have anything to do with me. Wives warned husbands that I was potentially dangerous – a marriage wrecker. I was to be avoided at all costs. Unexpectedly, I had at last attained notoriety. My bid for freedom was construed as an insidious contaminating disease capable of spreading to couples whose immune systems were weak.

Of course I was upset. I missed chatting on the phone to certain friends, gossiping about the affairs of other friends, planning social engagements and dinner parties, going to movies, concerts, curry dens and sushi bars. I had no one with whom to share exclusive recipes or to hunt down bargains in lesser-known boutiques. Most of all I missed the interminable exchange and competitive bragging about the exploits of our respective children and grandchildren. In our social circle we could not wait to tell each other about the exceptional successes of our children and the brilliance of our grandchildren's school achievements or sporting prowess. If we exaggerated slightly about their capabilities and potential, it was regarded not as being untruthful but rather as being hopefully optimistic. Until the disappearance of my friends I hadn't realised how much time I spent talking about my children and grandchildren. I suppose all of you should be rather relieved that you are no longer the focal point of my conversations.

Ah well, I learned a few things. I discovered how threatened people are by change. There is a certain stage in people's lives where they depend on having things stay the same, especially marriage. Divorce is an uncomfortable word and often has sinister connotations. I also believed, until that point in my life, that friendships are forever. But how ephemeral and fragile relationships really are!

But all that is too depressing to discuss with you while you are pregnant. You must have happy thoughts and be in a pleasant space, physically, mentally and spiritually, to produce a contented baby. I mean, when I was pregnant my mother-in-law used to tell me horror stories about the effects of watching movies with bad language and violence.

It's not an old wives' tale – there is truth in it. So remain calm and happy.

Much love
Mom

30 March

Dearest Rebecca

Your decision to come to Australia for the Batmitzvah and the reunion – brilliant! You find, amazingly, that the date seems to coincide with your vacation from the studio and your teaching commitments.

I am tickled pink that you have asked me what you should wear to the Batmitzvah. I never would have believed that I would hear such a question from you. Can I presume that you are finally taking an interest in clothes? Hard to believe. However, knowing how much you hate shopping, I am prepared to look for something suitable for you to wear. You might like to wear my 'no-nonsense' grey skirt and jacket that would do well for any occasion. Or, perhaps on your next visit we could even venture out together to buy something stunning for you. But whatever we decide, we can at last indulge in a bit of mother–daughter 'kugeling'.

I so vividly remember your rebellion in your teens, when your grandmother wanted to dress you up in feminine frilly dresses while all you wanted to wear were blue jeans and shirts. How you used to storm out of those boutiques in disgust! Your poor grandmother! She tried to encourage you to make the most of your good looks, to wear make-up and do your hair more stylishly. She herself was so elegant and fashion-conscious, and loved wearing beautiful things. How disappointed she was at your lack of interest in clothes and your appearance, when you shared so many other things – your passion for art, your love of colour, your ability to paint, your creative vision. I think she understood before anyone else that you were different, and although she tried to tell me then, I was so intent on defending your rights to your individuality that I never really heard her. I was also too busy trying to protect my mother from the harshness of the world. I did not want to cause her additional stress and anxiety, because of her poor health. Likewise she was always protecting me. It was a relationship based on real love and care and yet we played these ridiculous games of 'pretend'. And yet, when I was still a child I remember having the house filled with her bright intellectual gay women and men friends who came to dinner regularly without causing any fuss from my parents' other friends. Admittedly, while I was growing up I didn't realise they were different. I just preferred their company because they were fun, a bit kinder, and made me feel important.

I often wonder, if my mother were still alive, what she would think of your artwork now. You were such a brilliant colourist while you were growing up and your teacher Katerina was so proud of your achievements. Do you remember those brightly painted still lifes with orange pumpkins, red apples, burgundy aubergines and yellow peppers in wicker baskets on patterned tablecloths? Do you remember your clowns in their flamboyant costumes with their white mask-like painted faces? *Then* you were gay. Not now. The terminology is really weird because the young spontaneous artist of those days transformed herself into a sombre master printmaker who now rarely uses colour in her work and is content only when creating works in shades of black that rival Rembrandt's and Goya's darkest etchings and aquatints.

I know your work changed through those dark years of repression in the apartheid era when politicised art, literature and life went underground. I know that your involvement with the struggle and the draconian state of emergency imposed by the government to hide the atrocities that were being perpetrated influenced your vision of the role of art in society. I know, too, that you were no longer interested in art as decoration for the wall and that your purpose was to expose and transform. You have often told me that printmaking was the way to bring art to the people, being the least elitist and most accessible medium in which to work.

But have you forgotten the flowers, the sunrises and sunsets, the wondrous landscape of our country? Have you forgotten that people want to be happy and laugh? I mean, I do. Every time I look out of my window and see the changing seasons in the changing trees – the purple jacarandas in November, the yellow acacias, the pink cherry blossoms in the spring, the new green of the willow trees before their full burst into summer green, their autumnal transformation into orange and gold – I rejoice in the natural richness of colour and texture that surrounds me. I know you still enjoy the lovely things of life – you just don't choose to reproduce or interpret them in your prints. I wish your subject matter was not the harsh, the barren, the desolate, the burnt-out landscape. Where have the daisies gone?

I hope they will come back soon. Life without colour and laughter is too dreary. You need to lighten up more.

Much love
Mom

12 April

Darling Rachel

I do realise that you must be feeling marginalised with my constant chatter about the Batmitzvah in Perth, and I sympathise. Though I must say I have never understood why you have always felt left out of things simply because you were the fourth child, born ten years after your eldest sister. No amount of reassurance has ever convinced you that you were the most loved and spoilt of all my daughters. Perhaps that is why you are always trying to be different by doing something bizarre – to make us feel guilty.

What a pity you will not be able to go to Perth for the family reunion, though you have the most wonderful reason for not going. You are having a baby and I cannot think of a more joyous event. And I'm so grateful that the baby will be born before I leave for Australia. Perhaps you will then be able to find some space in your busy schedule so that I can spend time with you and have a meaningful mother–daughter encounter without me always having to resort to communicating with you via e-mail.

But what has got into you? What is the reason for your latest and most outrageous idea – your invitation to me and your sister Rebecca to the home birth of your second child? I cannot imagine that I will be able to attend. I will either be under heavy sedation or will, by the time your baby is due, be in the midst of my nervous breakdown. What has got into you, wanting your baby born at home when there are well-equipped maternity wards in hospitals all over the city? You have a choice of locality, doctors, nursing staff and whatever else is needed in sterile labour wards. But you intend having your baby in your bed – in your tiny little house with its uncarpeted wooden floors, red and blue walls, ethnic curtains, fertility objects and ugly masks on the walls. Is this what you want your baby to see as he/she comes into the world? It is quite preposterous, this peasant, earth-mother, uncultured experience that you call 'natural' childbirth. Midwives indeed! They went out of fashion half a century ago. Don't you know that we have arrived in the twenty-first century and there are people who have been specially trained for nine or ten years to become obstetricians and gynaecologists, qualified to employ procedures such as elective Caesareans and epidural anaesthetics to mitigate the horrid pain of childbirth?

I will have to have a serious discussion with your husband, who always seems to have a lot more sense than you do. I know that he wants to please you and go along with your crazy ideas, but this time you have overstepped the mark, my girl. I may even have to discuss this matter with your mother-in-law, for whom you have more consideration than your poor mother. Not that it matters what other people think, but how can I tell my friends, who are ultra-conservative anyway, that my daughter is having a *home birth*? I will be ostracised, laughed at, ridiculed – which, I am sure, will not even shake your obstinate resolve. Don't you realise that the first question I will be asked is which private clinic you are supporting and which fashionable gynaecologist is delivering your baby? Am I to tell my friends that you choose midwives because you prefer the time and energy they willingly give to help you through your labour? Do I explain to them that you prefer comfortable chaos to a clinically well-equipped, spotlessly clean environment for the birth of your baby?

I know that you will remind me that I was born at home. But it was different then. I was delivered by one of the most prominent women doctors in the country. It was a privilege to have Dr Mary Gordon agree to deliver a baby at home. Also, I was born upstairs in my parents' spacious bedroom, which was away from the rest of the house. Your open-plan living does not exactly allow for privacy and dignity. Well, maybe dignity is the wrong word, because giving birth is hardly conducive to dignified behaviour, what with all that moaning and pushing and heavy breathing. What on earth are you going to do about the neighbours? What if they hear about this primitive practice of having babies with midwives at home? What about your dog, who is always inside and on top of your bed? What are you going to do with Gideon? Is he going to be walking in and out of your labour room pushing his trains and trucks and flying his aeroplane? What will he tell his friends at school? I can't bear to think of the graphic description he will give to those innocent tiny tots at nursery school. Or maybe you are planning a water birth in that oversized old-fashioned olive-green bath in your eco-friendly organic-slated bathroom? It is too ghastly to contemplate. I mean, what would you expect me to do while you are giving birth? Perhaps some 'om' meditation on the floor will be soothing? I intend having full and frank discussions with my yoga teacher, my kinesiologist and my gynaecologist before uttering another word on the subject. I am sure that they are intelligent enough to have views that coincide with mine.

How can you show such lack of consideration for your mother's neuroses? I want the birth of your baby to be a happy event for all of us, not an existential happening only for you. I try so hard to accommodate and adjust to your nonconformist ideas and behaviour; yet this time I cannot see any logic in your decision. You are deliberately testing our relationship – expecting me to beg you to change your mind about the home birth, so that you can then accuse me of interfering in your family life. Well, if that's what it takes, I am prepared to beg. Please, have the baby in the maternity hospital.

Much love
Mom

14 April

My darling Leah

I am in shock. Your youngest sister wants to have a home birth.
Have you ever heard of anything more preposterous? You have
had six children and I'm sure the idea of having a baby at home
never entered your head. I know Sam would never have entertained such an idea. What do you think has got into your sister?
It's really too much for a mother to accept. Don't you agree?

This news has forced me to try and figure out what my four
daughters are really about. I mean, what changed you so much
after your immigration to Australia? Before you left, you were
carefree, full of fun and intent on having a good time. I admit that
your sense of responsibility and leadership skills were highly
developed, otherwise you would not have been head girl at your
school, but you seemed to combine your bubbly personality with
fun-filled activities. You loved parties, dancing, pop music, theatre, and you never missed a movie. Everyone enjoyed being
around you. I am not saying that has changed – people still love
being in your company. But it's all so serious now. Your friends
and activities are so respectable and 'worthy'. Nothing is frivolous.
Everything you do and say has a deeper meaning. You even managed to get Sam to follow your religious path. Before he married
you, he was so relaxed about everything and, like many of his

friends, attended synagogue only on the High Holidays. I know that after your Batmitzvah you asked me to keep kosher at home and I remember saying no to you. But I did add, rather flippantly, 'One day, when you get married, you can keep kosher.' Never did I imagine you would do so with such passion.

I need to remind you of a few things. Maybe they were never actually said before. When you were pregnant with Gavriela and decided to immigrate to Australia, I thought that my heart would break. I did not know how I would survive without you – my eldest daughter and my only son-in-law, on whom I relied completely. There was not a day that I did not visit your home and help take care of little Tzippy, my precious first grandchild. Rebecca was already out of the country, studying and working in America, and Sarah was completing her studies in London. Only Rachel was at home, still at school. I tried to make it easy for you by assuring you that I would never stand in your way if you thought your future lay in Australia. Your closest friends had already gone there or were ready to leave South Africa because of the political uncertainty and the bleak outlook. I sometimes wonder whether I could have prevailed upon you to stay.

I also wonder whether the shock of landing down under in an ex-convict colony turned you into a zealous community leader, determined to change the lives of ex–South African Orthodox Jews. You infiltrated homes, schools, charitable organisations, and the workplace by doing *mitzvot* for others. You showed yourself to be a caring, conscientious and reliable member of society, but what a price to pay! How do you think I feel about having this kind of exemplary role-model daughter? And with you being so far away from home your good deeds are magnified. My life is difficult enough without this added burden.

So, perhaps this is an opportune time for me to tell you exactly how I feel about your compulsion to feed the entire ex–South African Jewish community. Some mothers may be proud of the excellence of their daughters' traditional cooking and their competence in producing quantities of food for the High Holidays and other festive meals. But I am not one of those mothers. I suppose that is why I never hear anything directly from you. I am forced to hear the news from Sam's mother or even from people I don't even know.

I had a phone call the other day from a Mrs Rosenkrantz, or was it Mrs Rosenblum? Whatever her name is, she never stopped talking long enough for me to find out. She just went on and on about how wonderful and marvellous you are. She kept saying, 'Such a *balabos* – her chicken soup tasted like mine, her *kreplach* and *lokshen* pudding were made exactly the way I like it, and as for her *babkes*, they were exactly the way my Aunt Feigel baked them.' I didn't get a chance to ask her whether they were cinnamon or the ones stuffed with raisins and sultanas. But what really astounded me was when she told me that your hospitality to her and her family was a total surprise to her as you had never met them before. She casually mentioned how many people you'd graciously fed during those seven days in your *succah*. I was not only speechless but also horribly embarrassed. It was similar to the reaction I had when I heard about this past Rosh Hashanah, when you told me you were only having five or six different families for both nights, forgetting to mention that some families had six to eight children, while others had visiting relatives or friends with nowhere else to go. In the privacy of my bedroom, I counted the number of people sitting around your table and blushed. I think I also shed a few tears. Even now I cannot bring myself to say the number out loud.

What am I to suggest to you? Am I to join your circle of friends in telling you how generous you are to feed the Jewish population of Perth? Am I supposed to be bursting with pride that you, my eldest daughter, are earning the reputation of being the best kosher hostess in Western Australia? Well, I commend you for being so hospitable, for keeping an open house for all who need a place to eat and stay from time to time. I admire your energy, your capability and your capacity to juggle your family, charity work and studies to fit into your sixteen-hour day. But I have to suggest that you are in need of help, and this time I don't mean domestic help. Quite frankly, I think you need some serious counselling before your compulsion plunges you into a life of unmanageable chaos and ruin.

I need to take a break now before I say anything that may anger you.

Much love
Mom

16 April

Darling Leah

I've had a couple of days to cool down and think through what
still needs to be said.

As it was something I preferred to keep quiet, I don't know how
well informed you are about your family history. Your great-
grandmother on my side had twelve children – two died at birth –
and your paternal great-grandmother had eleven. At that time
large families were excusable. But those days have long passed,
and now people raise their eyebrows at numbers of children
exceeding four. Obviously there are exceptions, particularly where
your children are concerned. They, bless them, are exceptions to
any rule. But that has nothing to do with your troubled family
psyche. Your great-grandmothers and your grandmothers felt it
perfectly natural to sit down to meals with extended families and
hordes of children in order to fulfil their duties as homemakers.
Everyone was welcome in their homes. Amazingly, their poor circumstances did not appear to worry them, as no one ever seemed
to get up hungry from their table. Cooking and cleaning for their
ever-expanding families was what their lives were about. Today,
that kind of behaviour is considered barbaric, and I cannot bear
to think of my darling daughter constantly barefoot and pregnant,
following the outmoded lifestyle of her ancestors.

There has been a great deal of research on DNA lately, and it has been established that genes can skip a generation and suddenly manifest themselves in excess in the third and fourth generation. Thus I feel genetically responsible for the food bills that your husband has to pay. And so, my darling Leah, I, regretfully, am the one who has to make you face up to the realisation that you are afflicted by a psychological condition which, while not curable, can be kept under control. I am told on good authority that if you do not attend to it immediately, you and yours will all land up in the poorhouse. Your children will not be able to get the kind of education you want for them, nor will you be able to live in a nice suburb, drive nice cars and have nice friends. You have to realise that in time, no matter how hard your husband works, he will no longer be able to afford your addiction to feeding everyone you come across.

This may sound very harsh coming from your mother who loves you dearly, but if I can't tell you, who can? This is a disease that must be treated, like alcoholism, gambling or drug addiction. The first thing you have to do is to recognise it and admit that you have a problem. Let me be the first to apologise to you and confess my error in either praising or admonishing you for doing as much as you do. I realise now that you were and still are unable to help yourself. I admit that it becomes very difficult when your behaviour is praised, thus reinforcing the idea that you are doing an abundance of *mitzvot* to help others. How mistaken we were! You are a psychologically challenged do-gooder who cannot help your actions, and thus have to be treated by professionals who understand your complex psyche. The adrenalin rush that you get from doing a *mitzvah* is probably not as yet scientifically documented by psychologists, but let me assure you that besides making an interesting case study, it is an extremely serious health problem.

If we can get the right kind of help for you, and I have every confidence that we can, then not only will your condition be kept in
check, but great benefit will accrue to the Perth Orthodox community. All those aspirant do-gooders who yearn to entertain
overseas visitors, guide them on tours, hold lectures in their
homes, do cookery demonstrations, publish recipe books, organise women's groups for adult education, fund-raise for various
organisations, motivate for a new community *mikvah*, provide
Israeli dancing at the schools, arrange entertainment and catering
for functions, and feed their friends and relatives for the festivals
could then do so at last. They would no longer need to disap-
pointedly shake their heads with regret that 'Leah is doing it all'.
They too would get their chance. You would be making a sacrifice
for those women, who would then be able to demonstrate their
prowess in the kitchen and make their mark organising social
events. Let others aspire to win Woman of the Year awards. I
realise that at first it will be difficult for you to be a guest in someone else's house and to be in the audience at some conference you
previously organised, but you will have to find the strength and
courage to bear these ordeals. It is best for you and your community in the long term.

While I cannot help your husband financially to pay for psychotherapy, or whatever treatment you will need, I can assure
him, which I will do in a separate letter to him, that he will be
saving a great deal of money every month. Imagine the little
extras your family could enjoy if you were prevented from buying
in bulk at the supermarkets. Can you visualise the quiet and peace
that will descend on your household when you are able to sit
down to a Shabbat meal with your husband and children? There
are infinite possibilities for spending your time in pursuit of selfish pleasures. I have this pleasant picture of you relaxing in a

beauty salon enjoying a massage or having your hair, face and nails attended to. Remember that it is also a *mitzvah* to take care of yourself. Perhaps your therapist will suggest it as part of your recovery process. But do not mention that it was your mother who suggested this or anything else, as the therapist may want you to delve into the mother–daughter thing. These psych people are always blaming mothers for any problems they encounter.

Well, you are not the only one who can blame her mother. What about mine? She pampered and spoilt me and then expected me to know how to do everything. It's not as though she prepared me for life or gave me the tools to deal with the inevitable vicissitudes that life hands out. You can be sure she did not prepare me for marriage. How could she have allowed her precious daughter to be courted by an eligible bachelor eleven years older than her, wise in the ways of the world and at ease in the urbane sophistication that suffused his lifestyle? I mean, how was I supposed to resist being swept off my feet and courted on champagne and orchids, kept out dancing till dawn at nightclubs, wined and dined at the best restaurants or entertained by the rich and famous? Until then I had only dated university students in blue jeans and sandals who seriously believed they could change the world into a society where everyone was equal and happy, working towards utopia.

I blame my mother for not exposing me to a more worldly way of life. If I can't blame her, who can I blame? Although she did not approve of my marriage, because Marvin and I came from such different backgrounds, she told me repeatedly, 'You have made your bed, now you must lie in it.' And so I did, for thirty-seven years. I wonder what she would think of me now. She would certainly not have approved of my decision to divorce – very few people of her generation did. And yet she gave me the courage to do it. She gave me unconditional love and support in whatever I did. She taught me to cope with the good times and the bad. As a role model she was positive and ambitious. Had I not delved into this Freudian and Jungian psychology on the advice of your two sisters, I would never in my wildest imagination blame my mother for my problems. Because after all they are my problems – I am the only one responsible for them. But in the textbooks and on the couches of the psychoanalysts all our woes and troubles are directly attributed to the source: our mother. The good breast and the bad breast. My mother, being the eldest of ten, must have had only the good breast. That brief bonding with her mother before the other nine children came along must have been perfect! Isn't it quite absurd? All that stuff can drive you crazy. I shudder to think what my other daughters are saying about me.

Not you, Leah! I know that you have never felt the need to go to a clinical psychologist to hear nonsensical ramblings about your infancy and whether your mother bonded with you optimally. You were loved, adored, cared for and brought up as perfectly as possible. Ask anyone.

But of course you know that. You also know that whatever I tell you is for your own good.

Much love
Mom

22 April

My dearest Rebecca

It seems that Rachel's invitation to witness the birth of her baby
has shifted your way of thinking and prioritised your feelings
about being in Perth with your sisters, nieces and nephews as the
most important thing you could do right now. How delighted I
am. But I am so nervous about being present at the birth that I
am already having sleepless nights.

Isn't it strange that although we are living in the same country
now and are able to see each other more often, we continue writing to each other – e-mail now, instead of longhand letters on air-
mail paper. During those years that you were away in
Philadelphia, our letters kept us close and in touch with each
other's lives. I still have our correspondence, which was open,
spontaneous and real. Somehow it has always been easier for me
to write about feelings, emotions and ideas than to talk about
them. But I still would have preferred it if you were living closer
to me instead of in Venda doing all these community outreach
programmes and teaching at that Art Institute which you tell me
is so transformative.

But now back to the Batmitzvah! Of course I don't think there
will be any embarrassment or uncomfortable situations caused by

your bringing Trish with you to Perth, in spite of Leah and Sam's close involvement with the traditional Orthodox community. Their household is the centre for expatriate South Africans and so there is certainly no reason to expect that they would not graciously receive their extended family. Although, come to think of it, the political views of the expatriates have remained entrenched in the old South Africa, and they would certainly not have informed themselves about the inclusion of gender issues in our comprehensive and unique Constitution which even legalises same-sex adoptions, house ownership, bequests and life insurance policies. But you had better be prepared in case they demonstrate some surprise when Leah introduces you as her closest sister, her best friend, the godmother to her eldest son and the favourite aunt of all her children. In fact, your presence there may turn out to be the much-needed catalyst to change the narrow vision of some prominent members of the community.

One warning, though, for Trish. People here may know about her passion for cricket and her unbridled loyalty to and admiration for our cricket team, but I think it would be inadvisable for her to mention her opinions while in Australia. Sport can unleash all kinds of prejudice. I certainly don't want Trish's enthusiasm to precipitate arguments and bad feelings. It's quite extraordinary how disagreements about one's national team can lead to all kinds of violent incidents – I mean, look at the bloody British with their football teams. And it's almost as serious in South Africa, where neither political news nor crime statistics occupy the front pages of our newspapers. Cricket bosses, cricket captains, batsmen and bookies are the focus of our attention as the commission uncovers match-fixing, bribery and corruption. I should imagine that the Australians are very sensitive about these issues, particularly as the investigations haven't yet reached down under.

ſ

Aren't the priorities of people strange? The ex-pats in Perth are forever rationalising their reasons for leaving the country in which they were born, raised and educated – hardly ever acknowledging the money they made there, without which they could not have immigrated to a new country. They constantly defend their decision while extolling the virtues of their present lifestyle (no matter how awful it is). Most of the time, it doesn't make too much sense. So, on reflection, we had better be wary of them.

Much love
Mom

25 April

Dearest Leah

I had this odd e-mail from Rebecca expressing her concern about the reaction your friends and relatives may have to her and Trish's visit to you. I told her I couldn't imagine that your community, even though some of them are expatriate bigots and others are fairly orthodox and conservative in their views, would have any problems. What do you think?

But to be on the safe side, try and reread some of the books I sent you from that feminist bookshop in Philadelphia a few years ago. I certainly found them useful when trying to explain to certain people Rebecca's sexual preference for women. My favourite book was *Are You Still My Mother? Are You Still My Family?* I can still remember the way the author concluded the book:

> As you become more used to the idea of having a gay child you will probably find yourself so desensitised that your replies to questions will be rote. It might some day go like this at the bridge table:
> 'So when is Barbara getting married?'
> 'Probably never. She's a lesbian. Two spades.'
> 'Two no trump.'
> And the game goes on.

The other books were equally helpful and enlightening: *Twice Blessed: On Being Lesbian or Gay and Jewish; Different Daughters: A Book by Mothers of Lesbians*; and *Nice Jewish Girls*. What incredible stories these women have to tell! But can you imagine some mothers wanting to disown their daughters because they prefer women to men? Can you believe how bigoted society is and how it discriminates against gays and lesbians? I wonder if it is all really true. I'm sure it can't be that bad or that Rebecca had such a difficult time of it. The whole thing is probably exaggerated – I cannot imagine people being so prejudiced in this day and age.

Obviously there are exceptions. I have recently discovered that one should be circumspect with whom one discusses certain ideas, particularly if the group consists of narrow-minded ultra-Orthodox women in a Bible study seminar. The subject was the Book of Ruth, which I believe to be one of the gentlest stories in the Old Testament. In our discussion, I told the group about this amazing collection of stories and commentaries from a recent publication, *Reading Ruth: Contemporary Women Reclaim a Sacred Story*. In particular I mentioned the chapter by Rebecca Alpert, 'Finding Our Past: A Lesbian Interpretation of the Book of Ruth' – a well-researched study of relationships between women in Jewish texts, an approach which rarely receives prominence. If Ruth and Naomi were lovers, then the story can be interpreted as a Jewish lesbian Midrash. Alpert warns that the Midrash may distress certain readers, but I did not expect to be greeted by such a furore when I mentioned this interpretation to the group. They did not ask me to leave in so many words, but I had the distinct impression that if I again voiced these radical views I was no longer welcome.

You may be interested in hearing about some of my attempts

many years ago when I decided to come out of the closet about Rebecca. I invited my good friend Sybil to lunch, taking her to a smart northern suburbs restaurant where I told her about the interesting books I had bought in Philadelphia and how they had helped me to identify with other people in similar circumstances. I explained how relieved and pleased I was that I could now tell her why Rebecca didn't have any boyfriends. I am sure it had nothing to do with my confession when she suddenly choked on the spinach focaccia, turned red in the face, then became deathly pale as she mumbled her apologies and left the restaurant in a hurry. I pondered over her hasty departure while I finished my lunch and paid the bill. Having taken into account her unworldly views, I'd been both careful and diplomatic in breaking the news to her. It's not as though I suddenly burst out with the fact that my daughter is a lesbian. I'd broached the subject circumspectly and told her about some of the shocking reactions families and friends displayed when they discovered their daughters were different. I explained that they were still the same people but were different. I'm not sure Sybil understood the subtlety of the concept, but I can hardly believe it made an impact on our friendship or changed her opinion of Rebecca, whom she always admired. I think the reason we don't see much of each other anymore has to do with her over-conscientious involvement with her children and grandchildren, not to mention her demanding husband.

Funnily enough, though, when I told Hazel, whom I've known most of my life, she just looked at me and said in a straightforward matter-of-fact way: 'If it was my daughter, I would simply die of shame. And I would never tell a living soul, I would be so mortified.' But who needs her in my life? It's good riddance, I say. At around the same time, I recall telling my cousin Cheryl, who hardly blinked an eyelid and remarked, 'I'm sure it's just a phase and she will grow out of it. As soon as she meets a nice man she will get married and have kids.' She thinks Rebecca has been hanging out with the wrong crowd and still wants to introduce her to Solly's stepson, who is studying business science at Harvard. I told her I would ask her. Maybe he is also gay!

Much love
Mom

27 April

My dearest Sarah

Thank you for your Pesach and Easter greetings. I need some
cheering up. All the talk about Gavriela's Batmitzvah and the
prospective travel plans – who is coming and who isn't – I am
finding quite tedious. You haven't yet committed yourself, but I
am hoping you will be there. But right now I am worried sick
about Rachel's decision to have her baby at home. Do you think
she is serious or is she doing it to persecute me?

Yes, we really missed you at our seder table on both nights, reading the Haggadah, retelling the story of the Exodus, drinking the
four cups of wine, nibbling the matzo, singing the songs and
enjoying our festive meal. I know how much you would have
enjoyed the stuffed *kneidlach* and chicken soup, not to mention
the carrot and prune *tzimmes*, and the *klops* – which, if I say so
myself, were excellent this year. But to even the vegetarian you
have become, Pesach can bring a feast of meatless and fishless
dishes. Just before Pesach, Rupert, my non-Jewish friend who
enjoys our seders, gave me a book he found at an antiquarian
bookshop called *Jewish Cookery* by Leah Leonard. What a gem!
In it I discovered a recipe for meatless *rossel* borscht which you
would have loved. Although I was not able to soak the beetroots
for three weeks in a pickling jar, only to marinate them for three

days, the dish, which I garnished with minced parsley, diced cucumber and chopped hard-boiled egg, was, as my guests remarked, 'to die for'.

I'm glad that you celebrated Pesach even if it was in the English tradition, with thin clear soup and little balls that are more like dumplings than *kneidlach*. I presume they served turkey, roast potatoes and boiled carrots but forgot to prepare vegetarian dishes for you and Seja. The English do not associate themselves with the old style of Jewish cooking, judging from the food I have eaten in their homes. It is bland, tasteless and colourless. It does not feed a Jewish soul. Moreover, I'm sure that your homesickness was exacerbated by the London version of our traditional songs from the Haggadah – they are tuneless and formulaic, capturing none of the liveliness and fun we have in our communal singing. But a seder is a seder, and let's be thankful that you had one so that my darling Seja was able to meet her Jewish cousins.

And now, Sarah, I want to be frank with you. I have not criticised your child's nondenominational upbringing nor your husband's commitment to no religion. I have not interfered with you sending my granddaughter to a multicultural, multinational, multilingual pre-school. I think it's commendable that you are teaching her diversity. But now you have tried my patience and your luck too far. Why is Seja eating Easter eggs on Pesach and why have you taught her to call them Pesach bunnies? It's wrong, wrong, wrong. You are supposed to be telling her the story of the Exodus from Egypt, explaining about the plagues and why we eat matzos. Even the simple introduction to Pesach in the same *Jewish Cookery* book describes the background of the spiritual development and history of the Jewish people during the time of Pharaoh. We are reminded that Pesach has been referred to as the 'first general strike in recorded history' and the 'first organised flight for freedom from slavery'. With your political background and degree in labour relations you should be able to identify with this phenomenon and take it more seriously. By allowing Seja to eat Easter eggs over Passover, are you implying that there were little rabbits in the desert laying eggs covered in chocolate, and ignoring the serious plagues of frogs and other nasties inflicted on the Egyptians because they were idolaters? What is to become of her religious education, her roots and her heritage?

When I think of my four daughters attending the festival services at the Great Synagogue in Johannesburg, dressed alike in pretty dresses, hats, white socks and shoes, I cannot believe that you are not willing to continue this tradition. I was so proud to show off my model children to the congregation. You, Sarah, were always smiling, laughing and carefree – everyone agreed that you were a bright and beautiful child with the potential to be anything you wanted. We were the envy of the community with our strong feminine presence. Surely something rubbed off. I know how you hate me harping on your idyllic childhood and I'm aware that we are living in a different world now. But until now I have not objected to your burning incense while little Seja learns to chant mantras as you stand on your head like a yogi, but these Hindu practices are interfering with teaching her the important *mitzvah* of asking the four questions from the Haggadah.

I will not say another word on the subject – for now.

Much love
Mom

4 May

My darling Sarah

Well done! What a splendid decision to go to Perth for Gavriela's Batmitzvah! I am relieved that you were finally able to persuade Cedric, who is always so moralistic, to use the insurance money you got after those wily London burglars robbed you of your few possessions. After all, in the years Leah, Sam and their ever-increasing family have been in Australia, you have never managed to visit them there. Our reunions have always been here at home.

About Cedric's nervousness and ulcer attacks since your decision to go down under, I understand that he is not comfortable in family situations because he is shy and antisocial. Of course, it doesn't help his condition living in London, where being invited to tea on those rare occasions is a serious affair. You will have to convince him that staying in Leah and Sam's house with their six children, your sister Rebecca and her partner, Sam's mother from Johannesburg, together with me and my ex-husband (your father) sounds worse than it can possibly be. There is, after all, a guest suite for both of you and your adorable Seja, where you will have your own space and privacy. Cedric does not have to feel obliged to eat all his meals with fifteen other people who happen to be staying in the same house at the same time. You must convince him that you will have time to pursue your own activities.

Furthermore, you may explain to him that other people, and I'm specifically thinking of myself, will be much more uncomfortable than he is during those five days. I will be occupying a room with baby Shalom, his toys, mobiles, smelly nappies and frequent night calls. Sam's mother will be in a more privileged situation, sharing a room with the two older girls, while your father will sleep in relative peace and privacy in the downstairs playroom with the two dogs. Your sister Rebecca and Trish will be put up separately on mattresses in any room that has some floor space. We all need to make some sacrifices.

I want to talk of pleasant things, like our imminent reunion. I am aware that Cedric wanted to stay at a b. & b. while in Perth, and I heard how irate and insulted Leah became when she heard of it. She told me that as she is constantly putting up strangers in her house over Shabbat and the festivals, she does not understand Cedric's anxiety about the new experience of being in the midst of a warm, vibrant and loving – even if at times volatile and unpredictable – family. I realise that Leah can be overly enthusiastic, conscientious to a fault, and is inclined to be authoritarian. But then, I ask you, how else can her household function? Your Cedric will have to continue taking his Guronsan tablets and antispasmodic liquid, and do some deep breathing to endure the unavoidable onslaught on his body and mind. Who knows, he may survive it! You can assure him that he is not the only one who has had to go into therapy for this family meeting.

I am a Jewish mother so the rules are different for me. In fact they are different for each of my four daughters, who have chosen their own inimitable paths, each more weird and wonderful than the one before. My friend Gertie, who likes to think she is my therapist, told me what I already know:

South African Jewish mothers live on the edge. They have their children scattered all over the world and spend their lives chasing from one to the other. When they do get together they try so hard to make it all perfect that they botch it up. They have to squeeze a year or two into a month and then are surprised that their relationships with their children and grandchildren are somewhat fragile. And when they do get it right and they re-establish their bonds, it's time to leave again.

Could we have foreseen, when we brought up our children with strong family values in the warmth and comfort of their home, that they would disperse to various parts of the world to wrestle with social, economic and cultural problems and struggle to keep body and soul together? Did I imagine that my four daughters, who were such perfect children, would ever present me with such problems? What I need right now is less theorising and a quick-fix practical solution. We need to find a better way to interact in a confined space after being apart for so long.

I wonder if you even remember our calamitous reunion three years ago when we managed to snatch twenty-four hours together in Betty's Bay. You were en route to visit some projects in the Eastern Cape, Leah and family were having a beach holiday with us, while Rachel and Rebecca drove a thousand kilometres for the weekend. I had organised everything to the last detail as I wanted our time together to be just right. I had shopped and pre-cooked our dinner so that no one would have to spend time in the kitchen. I had prepared a fresh rock cod to cook on the braai while we sat having drinks outside on the patio. It never occurred to me that the fish would have caused such a domestic uproar. Sibling rivalry reared its ugly head as each of you wanted to show off your expertise in cooking fish on an open fire. It became a battleground for culinary power. Years of fighting for equal rights in the women's movement made your struggle for the dead fish quite militant. Five strong women (including me) – formidable in their own kitchens – behaved shamelessly. Needless to say the fish burnt and was inedible. Naturally, I took the blame. I admitted I should have known better and served an innocuous vegetable lasagne that none of us likes.

But with this impending reunion there is much more at stake. We are travelling great distances at great expense. We are going to be inconvenienced and uncomfortable – and I don't mean only our physical comforts. I, for one, am going to be put in the embarrassing and awkward situation of being with your father, whom I've only recently divorced because I don't want to be with him any more. Therefore, we need to orchestrate every event and eventuality in a mature way. We have to avoid communication breakdowns and lethal explosions when family feuds suddenly emerge from the buried past. I am depending on you because you have such great organisational skills.

If, dear Sarah, I am giving the impression that I am anxious about our get-together next month, I assure you the word anxious is a feeble substitute for what I am feeling. Terrified is more like it. However, you also know that I am an incorrigible optimist, with great faith. I am hoping that my children's capacity for humour and enjoyment, as well as their strong family feeling, will help us get through any tough situation. I need to believe that even if our reunion will be crazy, chaotic and potentially calamitous, it will be an extraordinary experience for all of us.

Let's come up with a game plan – or in your jargon, do some

'strategic planning'. I do not want arguments, surprises or compromising situations. And don't tell me to 'be cool' and take things as they come. You know I can't.

Much love
Mom

6 May

Darling Rebecca

You must have been in touch with Sarah, who told you how anxious I was feeling about the reunion in Perth. I'm sure you will all pull together to ensure that everything goes well. But I haven't said a word about my apprehension to Leah, so please don't mention it to her, Sam or the children. She will have enough to contend with.

You ask quite bluntly how it will be for me being with your father in the same house, sitting at the same table, travelling to the same places, doing the same things, sharing our children's lives for a time in a country that is not our own. Well, let me be equally frank with you. It may cause irreparable damage to mind, body and soul. I can hardly imagine what I will say or how I will behave at our enforced meeting. After thirty-seven years of marriage, it seems absurd that we will have nothing to say to each other after that dreadful divorce debacle. Decades of debris buried shallowly under an unsatisfactory divorce settlement is not exactly an arrangement that facilitates easy conversation. But having agreed to being there at the same time, I am sure that we are both mature enough to handle the situation and put on our happy masks for the celebration and the family photographs. We were always good at that.

Recently, I realised that indeed we were masters in the art of deception. No matter how we were feeling we were able to put on a cheerful disposition, especially for guests. I must say that Marvin was better at this game than I was because of his premarital experience in local theatre productions. I remember seeing him play the part of a villain in a murder mystery, and how much convincing it took before I agreed to go out to dinner with him. He was so mean on stage and yet, as I discovered, so charming in a social context. After we were married he was able to trivialise the most serious situations in our relationship by laughing and joking, so that it was almost impossible to tell that we were not the perfectly compatible couple. I found it difficult in those early years 'to put on a face' when I was so unhappy. But I learned that as Marvin's wife I dare not show what I was feeling. When I did, it was a betrayal, intolerable and unacceptable to him. His scorn was more unbearable than living a lie. In order to survive I had to learn to play the game, and I played it for nearly four decades, hoping the rules would change and the outcome would be different.

I presumed that most other couples were playing the marriage game by the same rules. In our circle of friends we were always dressing up and going out somewhere – where we went depended on what we wore and how we behaved. If it was out to dinner with the Rothsteins, Marvin wore a navy-blue suit, white shirt and a striped silk tie, while I wore an understated black designer outfit with all my good jewellery. If we were going to one of those intensely boring dinner parties with aspirant society friends who hadn't quite made it, I usually tried to make a statement by wearing something gaudy and extravagant to break the tediousness of the occasion. But I always dreaded those pretentious Sunday cocktail parties where the hostess specifically asked her guests to wear something 'casual'. One knew beforehand that everyone would be dressed to the nines. It always took great effort and a wild spending spree to look informally chic. One had to create the impression that it was effortless, as if one always 'hung around' in tight designer jeans with a studded leather belt and an expensive silk shirt.

Sometimes we staged fancy-dress parties with themes from the movies, which everyone loved. Do you remember *The Good, the Bad and the Ugly* party? No one came dressed as 'the ugly' – they were too busy being either very good or very bad. We rarely dressed for who we were – or, for that matter, spoke, acted or behaved as we felt. In fact, we were rarely what we seemed. And you know how Shakespeare dramatized that idea of 'seeming' in *Othello*. The play revolves around the notion that 'men should be what they seem'. The beautiful and passionate love story of Othello and Desdemona turns into a needless and heartbreaking tragedy as the cunning malice of Iago twists Othello's perception of faithful Desdemona's innocent action and transforms it into jealous rage. It's my favourite Shakespearean tragedy, yet each time I think of the tragic outcome I cannot help wishing they would have lived happily ever after.

Nothing as dramatic happened in our lives, yet by never revealing our true feelings or showing our real natures we found ourselves drifting into a situation where the flaws and deception slowly poisoned our marriage.

The Perth reunion will call for some play-acting from us. I hope I will remember my lines. But the event is too important not to succeed.

Much love
Mom

10 May

Darling Sarah

It seems that our upcoming reunion in Perth has sparked a sudden curiosity about my divorce. All of you are asking all kinds of questions, which quite frankly I feel reluctant to discuss. And, funnily enough, yesterday I bumped into Mildred, whom I haven't laid eyes on since my divorce. She had a hundred excuses why she hasn't contacted me, telling me how busy she's been and saying what a shock it was to everyone when my marriage dissolved. She told me that nobody would believe that Marvin and I actually split up and went through with the divorce. We were perceived as indestructible pillars of the institution of marriage – we were the perfect couple.

Some people have asked me, 'What took so long?' Others say, 'You stayed together so long, why couldn't you continue?' And then there is the question which I have asked myself many times, 'Why now – at this time of my life?' Well, I don't really have answers to these questions. It's all too complex, but if I were pressed for an answer, I would have to say that the timing was never right before. There were always other priorities – commitments to children, family and community.

While I was considering my options to get divorced, I read an article about a great Torah leader in the nineteenth century, Rabbi Israel Salanter, which may have influenced my thinking. In his reflections on his life, he explained that in adolescence he had aimed to change the world – to right the wrongs of humanity. But soon he realised he would have to change his own community first. Then he discovered he could do this only by changing his family – his wife and children. It took him many years to understand that his effort must be focused on changing himself, that to become a kind and decent human being was a life's worth of work. Only then could he contribute to his family, community and even the world.

I felt a resonance here with my own story. I too set out to change the world. I wanted people to live in peace with each other and their environment. I wanted to change the glaring injustices in our society – to recognise the humanity in all people, to allow people the opportunity to reach their potential, to eradicate poverty, prejudice and power. I wanted to change the views in my social circle – to encourage awareness, tolerance, generosity and a moral value system. I wanted my family to appreciate their self-worth and the worth of others. Most of all I wanted to change my husband into someone he could never become. Not even Torah scholars, Kabbalists, yogis or Buddhist monks would have set themselves such lofty goals and such idealistic expectations. I was living with my head in the clouds. It took me a long time to realise that the only person I could change was myself. And when that moment of truth finally dawned, there was no turning back.

I suddenly understood that I could not change Marvin's behaviour, nor did he want to change himself. He was content to live his life as he always had. He liked the routine of doing the same things, seeing the same people whose views were similar to his.

And I had validated this lifestyle by my tacit acceptance of it. In fact, most of us felt comfortable with it. But suddenly I could no longer live this kind of existence. My mind, body and spirit were stagnating – I was stifling. To survive, I needed to breathe, stretch and grow. The only path I saw open to me was to leave the marriage.

I still wonder if there was another way. I honestly don't believe so.

Much love
Mom

12 May

Rachel dearest

Obviously you are again feeling left out of things because you have been receiving messages from Sarah and Rebecca telling you that I am in a confessional mode and talking about my divorce, which all of you seem to find so fascinating. Well, let me assure you that if I were not going to be in Perth in a 'sharing mode' with your sisters, I would certainly not keep up this correspondence of enlightenment. I also think you should occupy your mind with more pleasant things and concentrate on the practical details of having a baby.

Have you found curtains for the baby's room? Did you finally find time to sort out Gideon's baby clothes, vests and blankets so that you can reuse them for the new baby? Most things should be in good condition, but they need to be washed and freshened up. Did your friend Susan return the cot and pram you lent her? Is Eli still attending prenatal classes with you? Is he still feeling positive about the idea of a home birth? Maybe he is having second thoughts. What have you done about cutting down on your clients and your workshops? You must prioritise your activities. And why are you now wasting time sitting at the computer waiting to receive e-mail from your mother and sisters?

I have this weird feeling that you are trying to analyse me and do a psychological assessment on my reasons for divorcing your father. You keep wanting to pinpoint the exact circumstance leading to my decision. You ask, 'What was the last straw?' and 'What pushed you over the edge?' And, that quintessential question psychologists ask, 'How did it make you feel?' Those questions really annoy me, and you know that I stopped going to that nice clinical psychologist years ago because I was so peeved by her pathological need to know about my feelings. I suppose I should be grateful that you are a play therapist and not a sexologist who would not only scrutinize the sexual aspects of my marital relationship but would find Freudian sources in my subconscious alter ego that have precipitated my life-changing behaviour.

Well, there was no sudden revelation or out-of-the-ordinary happening. Your father did not suddenly announce that he had fallen in love with another woman and was going to ride off with her into the sunset. And conversely I had no thoughts of exchanging my husband for another. I sometimes wish it had been that simple. In fact, it was a series of events over a long period of time that ultimately led to our divorce. I don't intend to list them because it really doesn't concern any one of you. The relationship between married couples is complex and I find the topic embarrassing to discuss with my children. I would think most couples – even the psychologically enlightened ones – would shy away from a heart-to-heart parental confession. Or is it my own inability to confront the real issues? My feelings are still raw and I'm feeling too vulnerable to expose them. Nor do I want to point fingers at your father's weaknesses and my own – as well as my inability to deal with them.

If you want to pinpoint the incident, it was our reunion at Betty's

Bay for your father's birthday bash. The catalyst was his speech to his family and friends, when he announced: 'From now on, I am going to do things "my way", à la Frank Sinatra.' I was totally baffled by this unexpected statement and couldn't help wondering where I had been for the past thirty-seven years to have missed something as obvious as the fact that Marvin was not living his life exactly as he wished. He then elaborated his plans: 'Now that I have retired from the rat race in Johannesburg I have decided to accept this great offer from Barnaby and Myrtle to help set up several b. & b. establishments along the Cape coast. They are convinced that my business skills, my knowledge of food and wine, and my contacts in the tourism industry will be invaluable for their venture. I have no doubt that Mom will love the idea of moving out of the concrete jungle to the Cape and will enjoy everything this lifestyle offers, far from the crime and violence of city life. I haven't told her as yet, because I wanted to surprise her. But now that the deal is done and everything has been arranged, it will be great fun for our friends and family to visit us often. They will be able to spend weekends and holidays with us drinking the best wines, eating gourmet food and enjoying the many pleasures of the Cape.'

Luckily I was sitting down when your father made his speech. Otherwise I'm sure I would have fallen flat on my face. I wondered whether this was another of his hare-brained schemes, but I soon realised he was deadly serious. Everyone at the party was cheering and congratulating him on his decision. They all agreed it was a perfect plan, the right place for Marvin to be, a fine opportunity to use his talent and skills as a professional host. I closed my eyes for a few seconds, visualising my role in his new venture. I pictured myself in a frilly white apron and towelling headband busily working behind the scenes: preparing a sumptuous breakfast for the guests, anticipating their every need; placing a basket of seasonal fruit, freshly baked rolls and a tasteful vase of fresh flowers on each table (not forgetting a bottle of Pinotage wrapped discreetly in a patterned dishcloth); then rushing upstairs with my broom, mop and duster to clean the rooms and put freshly laundered linen on the beds. I imagined myself as Mrs Fawlty in *Fawlty Towers*. I don't know whether I giggled, shuddered or groaned aloud, because Marvin and his friends gave me disapproving looks. As I was told later, Marvin was confident that he would be able to convince me of the merits of his grand plan.

It was then that I knew with certainty that I was not prepared to surrender the rest of my life to the pursuits of the hedonistic lifestyle my spouse wanted. I was tired of the masks, dressing up, the parties, the 'morning-after-the-night-before' hangovers, the constant need to entertain and be entertained, the pretence of having fun, and the repetitive mindless chatter among people with whom we associated. I preferred being on my own with my books, music and meditation. I craved silence and solitude. I would refuse to fulfil his expectation 'to go wherever he goeth'. This time my place was not going to be beside him, whatever he chose to do or not to do. I had no intention of leaving my home in Johannesburg, a city that energised and defined me. I did not want to be with a man with whom I was no longer able to share my thoughts, my feelings, my pain and my joy. Years ago we had lost the art of communication, and with it the feeling of mutual respect. The things that kept us tied together were the children, grandchildren, friends and the habit of being married. I had been clinging to my comfort zone out of fear of the unknown. But without the familiar props, what was the purpose?

It took the event of our reunion to understand that the time had come for me to say 'No more', to step away and get out of a situation I had not been comfortable in for a very long time. A perfect opportunity had presented itself. The timing was right and my decision was not going to cause upheavals or traumas in the lives of my daughters and their families. I felt the need to extricate myself from the role of good wife, mother and support system, in order to find out who I am, and to find the real essence of my existence. The only thing I was sure of was that I wanted to move on and live my life differently – according to my own conscience.

Does this answer some of your questions?

Much love
Mom

13 May

Dearest Leah

Most of the time I am really thankful that you are so close to your sisters. Right now, however, I'm not. I wish you would stop sharing information about me on e-mail. What I have told Rachel in confidence seems to be immediately relayed to you and your sisters. I am finding the dissemination of this information awkward and uncomfortable. It is also raising many questions that up to now I have not felt like answering. I don't quite know what to do. Ride with the storm or run for shelter? I got myself into this mess, so I had better see it through. Fortunately for me you are a good listener and seldom judgemental.

The path of self-discovery is a scary one, filled with doubts and uncertainties. Often I did not like what I saw when facing myself in the early hours of the morning, alone and alienated from everyone who had made up the fabric of my life. It would have been an easier and more accommodating decision to surrender to the continuing merry-go-round of my marriage. Divorce was a seven-letter word frowned on by our community. But the sudden notion that I had a choice, the option of an alternative way of living the rest of my life, gave me a surge of energy and purpose that helped me through the barrage of obstacles and difficulties that lay ahead of me.

In hindsight, I wonder how I managed to stay on course and get through the awful process of divorce. In fact, while sitting alone in the divorce court, waiting for my case to be called and hearing some of the distressing stories of marriages that had gone horribly wrong, I felt like jumping up and shouting that I had made a terrible mistake and did not want my marriage to be ended in this cold and impersonal atmosphere by a hammer blow from a faceless judge. I had put in too much time and energy. But I sat it out, knowing deep down inside of me that I could no longer live a lie.

The day of my divorce was not terribly out of the ordinary, except that it seemed to stretch out interminably. After having a celebratory cup of coffee in a cracked mug in a downtown coffee shop with my advocate, I did not feel like doing much for the rest of the day. I felt uncomfortable about phoning my children to give them the tidings, uncertain whether they would consider them good or bad. I couldn't phone my friends, because by that stage I had alienated all of them by going through with the divorce proceedings. I could not think of anyone who would understand why I insisted on the drastic measure of a Supreme Court decree. The reality was that I had no friends in whom to confide or on whom to lean for support. I could have plunged into a severe bout of depression. I briefly considered having that nervous breakdown I was always threatening to have when my children were troublesome or my husband was particularly obnoxious. Instead I went to the movies – a cure for all, especially as I managed to see two infinitely forgettable Italian films at the foreign film festival.

I think I handled the civil divorce in an exemplary way. No shady areas for analytic burrowing into my psyche. Don't you agree?

I did not handle myself quite as well in procuring the Jewish *get*.

That was an ordeal I don't want to go through again. The emotional enormity of obtaining a writ of divorce from the Beth Din – the Jewish court of law – was soul-wrenching. I phoned my friend Zelda from our synagogue and begged her to come with me. I was shaking so much she had to drive my car. I clung to her as though she were my mother, even though she is ten years younger than I am. One of the rabbis I encountered there was your *cheder* teacher – he taught you all Hebrew from the age of six. I'm not sure who was more embarrassed, he or I. But he was kind and caring and helped me get through my ordeal.

I had tried to prepare myself and had read a fair amount about this process. However, the only book that made sense to me was one written by the rebel *rebbetzin* Blu Greenberg, *How to Run a Traditional Jewish Household*. She explained it in a practical way: 'It is the man who gives the writ of divorce to the woman who accepts it in the presence of two witnesses.' Well, my man was in Betty's Bay. It had to be done on his behalf. According to Greenberg, it is not an adversarial proceeding – no reasons need be given, and there is neither fault-finding nor a financial settlement. All of that is taken care of at some previous time. I was not sure whether this knowledge was a comfort or an additional distress for me. I intuitively knew the procedure would be neither simple nor easy.

A scribe had written the writ on behalf of Marvin, and I was asked whether I would accept it of my own free will. Those present were asked whether there was anyone who wished to protest. Finally three rabbis of the Beth Din signed the writ. I was required to hold up the *get*, walk a few paces, return, and hand it back to the officiating rabbi. He then proceeded to tear the four corners of the handwritten document so that it could not be used again. The solemn procedure witnessed by three bearded rabbis in the hushed room was my farewell, psychologically, emotionally and spiritually, to my husband whom I had sworn in a synagogue thirty-seven years previously to cherish, honour and obey.

When we walked out of the building the sun was still shining. It was a glorious autumn day. I had a new status: I was now a Jewish divorcee. I did not know how I felt about that. I suppose a bit numb.

I drove Zelda to her work, which was not far from the Beth Din, thanking her profusely for being with me. But driving home after my ordeal, I must have been in an altered state of consciousness. It is hardly surprising that my mind was far away and my thoughts jumbled. My stomach hurt and my heart was racing. Emotionally I was on a roller coaster – suddenly soaring up, then plummeting down, and finally hitting the ground with a thud. It was as though I was driving my car on automatic pilot, negotiating the corners, avoiding other cars, changing gears, and braking at stop signs. While waiting for a traffic light to change to green, my foot inexplicably came off the brake an instant too soon – with the result that I gently bumped the car in front of me. It was a mere touch. I put my head out of the window and apologised profusely to the driver with smiles and hand gestures. He seemed to accept my error of judgement with good grace.

I have no idea how it happened, but at the next stop light I accidentally touched his car again with my front bumper. This time he leapt out of his car, gesticulating in the most ungentlemanly fashion, and ordered me to pull over to the side of the road. Of course, I complied. He forced me out of my car with a bombardment of expletives such as I had never heard before. He yelled at me at the top of his voice and made rude signs which profoundly embarrassed me. Shaking uncontrollably, I kept my voice calm and apologised once more, agreeing that it was my fault but pointing out how fortunate we both were that it was such a mild bump that no damage to his car had occurred. Had I punched him in the mouth, he could not have not have reacted more abusively. He continued to castigate me until he finally calmed down enough to demand my details – my license, address, phone number, insurance company, and every credit card I had in my wallet, including my over-sixty movie card. He finally threatened me with insolvency when the damage to his new yellow Porsche, which he had just driven out of his dealer's garage, was assessed. Beside myself, I even resorted to tears as I implored him to look at his car, which, I kept assuring him, did not have a mark. He eventually drove off, telling me that he was going to have the car inspected by the dealer.

I wondered whether to return to the Beth Din and explain to the rabbis that my *get* was not serving me well, since I might have to serve a term of imprisonment for not having sufficient funds to respray and recondition the body of the yellow Porsche back to its pristine state. I phoned my insurance agent, financial advisor and bank manager to alert them to my possible impending insolvency. I discovered that I no longer had insurance on my car. Before the divorce was final Marvin had cancelled it. My head was pounding as I closed the curtains in my bedroom, crawled under the covers and prayed that all the events of the day were a bad dream.

I should have had more faith because a few hours later the owner of the yellow Porsche phoned to tell me that his car was undamaged. He even apologised for his abominable behaviour and foul language. After breathing an enormous sigh of relief, I thanked him profusely for his phone call, then plucked up enough courage to ask him why his road rage had been so intense. His story was simple. He'd thought I was trying to hijack his new car. It seems that one of the methods hijackers use is to bump the car several times before taking illegal ownership. I was flabbergasted. Imagine someone mistaking me for a dangerous criminal! I hardly knew whether to be flattered or insulted. It certainly gave my flagging ego a boost. I was not simply a new divorcee, a victim of circumstance, an over-sixty woman with an uncertain future, I was someone to be reckoned with. A potential mobster with pretensions in the designer car world – someone with good taste and a penchant for custom-made cars worth over half a million rand.

What do you think of your mother now? I'm no pushover. And I'm certainly not a candidate for an in-depth psychoanalytic session on someone's couch. I might have attained a certain notoriety from this incident had it not resolved itself so undramatically.

I'm sure there is a lesson in all this, although I'm not sure exactly what it is. How is it possible that a trivial incident like bumping a car, even if it is a yellow Porsche, and the prospect of paying vast amounts of money to a spoilt rich stranger can take precedence over the most serious and momentous event of my life – the Jewish divorce from your father?

Much love
Mom

15 May

My darling Sarah

So, Rachel told you about my little run-in with the yellow Porsche. I admit that I was distraught at the time and imagined myself languishing in a first-offender's prison cell after losing a lengthy court case to that rich, foul-mouthed, ill-mannered, irate owner of that squashed-in sardine can that costs as much or more than a house. Yes, I suppose I was lucky that I did no real damage to his car and that he did not become violent.

However, the emotional cost was almost as much as the financial cost. The incident forced me to attend to my financial affairs – something I had never done before. Do you think it absolutely necessary to have insurance? I know most people have it, but one needs to have a B.Com. degree to fill out those incomprehensible forms written in appalling jargon. They made me feel like a complete idiot! And it's so expensive! I recall my first meeting with Bruce, a financial consultant recommended to me to take care of all my financial worries. It was a most unpleasant experience, as he was patronising to the extreme. He even had the effrontery to tell me that I would have to pay for his expert advice and services – as though I thought he was doing it out of the goodness of his heart. In a matter-of-fact way he told me that he would invest my savings on the stock market, as he feels sure it will recover shortly.

He was dismissive of my apprehension and my poorly informed remarks about frequent market crashes and devaluation of our currency. He assured me he knew what he was doing. If, then, I have nothing to worry about, my money is safe in his capable hands, and I have ample insurance on my house, my car and my life, why do I feel so uneasy?

At the moment I must be feeling oversensitive because I did not like your rude reminder and insinuations about that period in my life when I was actively engaged in a war on Volkswagens. I think you exaggerate. Anyway, it was different in those days. Admittedly, I expressed my overt prejudice about buying German goods. But you are right in some respects – my focus was particularly on the hapless Volkswagen, especially the green ones – and at the time there seemed to be many on the road. I suppose I was fortunate that there were no Porsches around and that road rage had not become hazardous to human life. Otherwise, I would certainly not be here to tell the tale.

You must understand that I didn't set about it deliberately. Mostly it was an unconscious act which I often regretted, especially that time when I reversed into a stationary Volkswagen at the cemetery. It happened to be the only car parked in the grounds when I went to visit your grandfather's grave on the anniversary of his death. But I simply did not see it. It was green and parked near some bushes under a tree. When I reversed into it, the owner, who worked in the office of the Chevra Kadisha (the Jewish burial society), heard the bang and came rushing out shouting, 'I saw you do it, I saw you do it.' Of course I did it. There was not another living soul there and I have always wondered whether he thought I was going to deny it. As I was so embarrassed about the incident, I didn't tell anyone about it and paid for the damages and the cost of hiring a car for Mr Blumgard on a budget plan out of my housekeeping money.

You unkindly reminded me of another incident that happened years back, as you said it was similar to the yellow Porsche story. Well, it was completely different. In those days people who drove cars were well-mannered and considerate, and gave the benefit of the doubt to an unwitting perpetrator of a minor offence. Then, too, there were extenuating circumstances and the story should be seen in the social context of the time and place.

It happened when I was driving to the city on a hot summer's day. The traffic along Sauer Street, my favourite route into the city, was moving at a snail's pace because of some building construction. I was adjusting the dials on my radio because of the noise when I suddenly felt a bump. I looked up and found that to my surprise I had ever so lightly hit a car in front of me. It happened to be a green Volkswagen. Admittedly, at the time I had an intense dislike of green Volkswagens, but that is not why I hit it. I flashed the driver one of my dazzling smiles, shrugged and mouthed an apology, which he graciously accepted. During the next ten minutes we covered only about three city blocks, and I was watching a gigantic crane overhead lifting some huge blocks of concrete onto the building site when I felt my car lurch forward and come to rest on the rear bumper of the car in front of me – the green Volkswagen. I grinned sheepishly at the driver, waved to him and showed him with sign language how embarrassed I was. Again he graciously accepted my apology. After several minutes of concentrated driving I was disturbed by the sight of a city landmark being demolished – another familiar feature vanishing. When I felt my car lurch forward, I knew, with a sinking feeling, that I had again hit the green Volkswagen. This time the driver got out of his car, leaving the engine running, approached my open window and politely said, 'Lady, what is it you don't like about me? You have hit my car three times in fifteen minutes.'

'It's nothing personal,' I assured him. 'My foot keeps slipping off the brake. It could be my shoes, the heat or this hang-up I have about green Volkswagens.'

'I have a suggestion,' he said. 'As this is the only car I possess and I like it, I am going to stop the traffic while you move into the other lane to avoid further temptation.'

I was impressed with his good sense and excellent manners and proceeded to follow his suggestion. Ignoring the hooting of the other cars, I changed lanes in my bid for freedom. As I turned to offer a farewell wave to my victim, I heard a sickening scrape of metal. I had achieved the impossible. I had hit his car again.

Recalling this story, I have a strange feeling that my dislike of Volkswagens, my hostile attitude to Germany and my involvement with the literature of the Holocaust are linked to the breakdown of our relationship. You, unfortunately, are only too aware of the arguments that took place in our house over the years because of my personal campaign never to buy goods made in Germany. Naturally it created problems in my marriage because Marvin did not share my views – neither, in fact, did his family nor our circle of friends. They preferred to buy the best – German cars, German appliances, German fabrics, German electronic equipment – from pencils and make-up to wine and airline tickets. Marvin visited Germany to conduct business with certain German manufacturers – even during our honeymoon – and brought me gifts from his trips that were like knives in my back.

But I'm more tolerant now. I have worked through much of my anger and even have some German friends for whom I have great respect.

No more about that now, however. There is much to look forward to, and you will have to start preparing yourself, Cedric and Seja for the long trek to Perth. I can't wait to put my arms around you.

Much love
Mom

17 May

Dearest Rebecca

You will never guess with whom I have just had lunch at the Rosebank Hotel. Gus and Sadie Axelrod! As you know, they have been living in Israel for several years but have now come back to settle in Johannesburg. They are dear friends and, apart from their right-wing politics and their occasional 'holier-than-thou' attitude, I really like them and we have maintained a healthy respect for one another. They were absolutely shocked to hear of my divorce. They had lost touch with the friends Marvin and I had in common and so they hadn't heard the news. Quite surprising, don't you think, in a society that thrives on gossip? They then told me their news. You will never guess. Cynthia has just married a Hindu! Can you believe it? One of the main reasons the Axelrods immigrated to Israel was because Cynthia was searching for her identity. She apparently found it in a yeshiva in Jerusalem. But after a few years she wanted to come back here and do a postgraduate degree in poverty alleviation in Third World countries. (And we know all about that here, don't we?) Anyway, during her course at university, she met this divine Hindu professor who teaches in the history department, and they fell in love. When they decided they wanted to get married, Sadie and Gus came rushing back for the wedding. And here they'll stay. As they said to me, 'It no longer makes sense for us to go back to Jerusalem.

And, we've learnt a tough and expensive lesson – it's foolhardy to follow your children.' That's so true. I know many parents who have come crawling back after their children upped and left wherever they were for greener pastures. I, for one, am delighted they are resettling in Johannesburg, as I can do with a few of my old friends around me. They have promised to introduce me to Ugesh because I would love to have them all for a Shabbat meal.

We chatted about old times and the fun we had when we travelled overseas together. We got on so well together – Marvin and Gus seemed to enjoy each other's company, and Sadie and I certainly had some good times in the shops and art galleries. It was quite astonishing that when your father and I were away from home, especially on holiday trips, we got on brilliantly together. We put aside all our problems and enjoyed visiting places we had never been to before. We loved meeting people and took advantage of the sights, the culture, the food and the life we encountered wherever we went. We often wondered why our relationship flourished so strongly when we were far from home.

The Axelrods naturally wanted to know all about you and how you like being back in South Africa after your long exile in Philadelphia. They remember visiting you in your tiny apartment in that derelict building while you were studying. Sadie was particularly surprised to hear that you had chosen to live and work in Venda after being in the U.S.A. for so long. After all, it's not exactly the hub of a First World culture – or, for that matter, the centre of the visual arts. I told her it was a temporary measure and that I was sure you would be back in Johannesburg soon. Maybe that's wishful thinking on my part, but your talents are wasted teaching at that bankrupt Art Institute, and I'm sure you can find other people to run those outreach projects in which you are so involved. I am also sure that you and Cynthia can resume your friendship where you left off as teenagers. You had so much in common then.

I must confess it was a difficult time being your mother during the eighties when you lived in that bleak apartment block with Georgina. At first I was pleased that you had a companion, that she was Jewish and came from a nice middle-class family. I remember telling my friends how fortunate it was that you had been awarded a bursary for your postgraduate studies, although I didn't always elaborate on the various jobs you took to pay for your rent, food bills and books. But I think you learnt a lot working as a waitress, bartender, house painter, cleaner and odd-job/maintenance person. You were young and idealistic, and I believed it strengthened your resolve to succeed in the real world.

I am sure you were aware that on my visits to Philadelphia each year I led a double life. My role as a Jewish mother was quite onerous because I felt I had to be supportive of you and Georgina to lighten the burden of your lives. I can now admit to you that I had huge problems adjusting to your lifestyle. Each time I entered your apartment I became thoroughly depressed and wanted to run away. The neighbourhood was depressing, the building you lived in was ugly and your apartment gave me the creeps. I don't know why Georgina insisted on plastering her disturbing paintings on every wall. I realised her artworks were expressions of the way she was feeling and reacting to the brash American culture, her homesickness and other complex problems. But I found it self-indulgent the way she inflicted her pain on others, especially her graphic depiction of illness – blood-red acrylic paint interspersed with black blobs and bile-green squiggles. Ugh! Perhaps an art therapist would have found her work revealing and courageous, but it made me nauseous. If she had to express her misery, she should have done it in a therapy situation and not in a place where one eats, sleeps, works, relaxes and entertains dinner guests.

Your relationship with Georgina was a prickly subject I was never able to discuss with you. I bent over backwards trying to be sympathetic to her woes and troubles and attempted to understand her work. But those disturbing images on her canvases kept me awake at night – her outpourings made me feel suicidal. Her art was not a process by which she was healing herself. It became an end in itself, growing, expanding and stretching its tentacles to smother and consume any healthy living creature in its path. I became convinced I was the victim in this drama and that Georgina's prolific output was her way of torturing me before getting rid of me. This became overwhelmingly clear the night I came to dinner in your chamber of horrors, when I almost choked on the fumes of the wet paint of her latest work which hung menacingly above my chair, threatening to drip onto the food I was eating. I am sure you don't even remember the incident. But I could not control my despair. I burst into tears, fled the apartment and threatened never to return.

Of course I did return – the following day. Although I could not bear the thought of you living in that oppressive atmosphere, I did not want to appear to be small-minded and prudish by revealing my disapproval. I needed to show you that I did not mind the sparse furnishings you had randomly picked up from garage sales or from the pavements on Tuesdays when people discarded their unwanted household possessions. It had nothing to do with my self-confessed snobbishness that I wanted a more respectable lifestyle for my daughter. I assured you that I found your original and eclectic way of furnishing the apartment quite interesting –

the moth-eaten old couch, the sixties lamp, the wooden table, the odd Victorian chairs, the black lacquered cupboards, the coat-stand where you hung your pots and pans, the orange floral carpet, and the worm-eaten four-poster bed. It was certainly a functional and cost-effective way of furnishing. I consoled myself with the thought that as more pavements yielded up their treasures, your furnishings would gradually change and become more cohesive.

It is only now that I can admit to you that had I not had my luxurious accommodation with our cousins, well-to-do Philadelphians in their leafy suburb, I might not have made such frequent trips to see you. My other self revelled in the tastefully furnished space they made available to me. How I appreciated their superb artworks, antiques and all-American appliances in their gracious home. Travelling on my own, unencumbered, free of responsibility, I was determined to make the most of the cultural life of the city. When we met on neutral ground, I could indulge you in the luxuries of going to concerts, galleries, museums, theatres, movies and wonderful restaurants.

Likewise, you pandered to me by encouraging me to go on all those whale-watch trips out of Plymouth in Cape Cod, a relaxing train journey from Philadelphia. I was never quite sure whether you used seasickness as an excuse to have time out on your own, or whether you thought my compulsive behaviour to watch whales bizarre. Ever since embarking on my study of *Moby Dick* – and following it up with a pilgrimage to New Bedford and Nantucket – I, like Ishmael, have 'swum through libraries and sailed through oceans' in search of the inscrutable, unknowable White Whale. It was my way too of 'driving off the spleen, and regulating the circulation'. It became my therapeutic escape from situations I wanted to avoid: 'Whenever I find myself growing grim about the mouth; whenever it is a damp and drizzly November in my soul; whenever I find myself involuntarily pausing before coffin warehouses, and bringing up the rear of every funeral I meet; and especially whenever my hypos get such an upper hand of me … then, I account it high time to get to sea as soon as I can.'

Being a Jewish mother, wife and grandmother, I could not simply go to sea whenever I felt the need. Yet when I was in Cape Cod I often did, and I became friends with several marine biologists who were researching the habits of the humpback and fin whales in Stellwagen Bay. I was even persuaded to adopt a whale. Having presumed, for some unknown reason, that my new 'child' was a male, I told whomever I could that I had a son at last! Until one year, when Spoon showed up with her calf Regalis, and to my embarrassment, my status changed – I became an adoptive grandmother.

With every whale-watching excursion I undertook my passion, fascination and curiosity about whales grew. As one of Melville's characters in *Moby Dick* remarks, 'Any way you look at it, you must needs conclude that the great Leviathan is that one creature in the world which must remain unpainted to the last.' The only way of finding out what a whale really looks like is to go whale-watching. Poor Ahab – in his monomaniacal attempt to hunt down and kill the White Whale, he and his crew went down with the *Pequod* and only Ishmael was saved to tell the tale. But now, a hundred and sixty years later, Ahab has been resurrected again by a wonderful author named Sena Jeter Naslund, who has written a companion piece to *Moby Dick* called *Ahab's Wife*. Imbibing the spirit of Melville and of mid-nineteenth-century New England, she has re-enacted the adventure. But it is Melville's omniscient narrator who has the last word in the majestic conclusion of *Moby Dick* with the unforgettable image: 'Now small fowls flew screaming over the yet yawning gulf; a sullen white surf beat against its steep sides; then all collapsed, and the great shroud of the sea rolled on as it rolled five thousand years ago.'

My whale-watching escapades were curtailed when you finally made the decision to come back home after spending nine years establishing yourself as an artist and teacher in Philadelphia. Of course, I was pleased – not about forgoing my journeys out to sea but about your return to South Africa. I knew you were homesick, not only for your family and friends, but for the people, the taste, the smell and the energy of Johannesburg. You never felt comfortable with American Coca-Cola culture; your mind and heart were always in Africa. I understood your longing to put your feet down on African soil, feel the warmth of the sun on your back, breathe in the rich colours of the landscape and live among the people who were familiar to your life experience.

But I was so preoccupied with my expectations of your homecoming that I lost sight of the fundamental motivation for your return – your commitment to work towards a democratic transformation in South Africa. Nor had I taken into account that your nine years of independence in Philadelphia had changed the dynamics of our relationship. My seemingly tactful and discreet behaviour on my visits to you in Philadelphia hardly fooled you as to my real intentions as a conscientious Jewish mother. Had I suspected that you were not still the girl I imagined you to be, would I have put myself in the embarrassing position of making elaborate preparations for your homecoming? But I had no reason to expect that you would sabotage my meticulous arrangements. I had found a charming, fully furnished garden cottage for you and reserved a modest studio where you could work and teach while re-establishing yourself on the local art scene. I had invited several interesting and well-connected people, including some of your friends who had become professionals in promising careers, for a drinks party to launch your career after your long absence. I even planned the menu to include some of your favourite food. When you shook your head and said no to me on all counts, I was flabbergasted. What I had done wrong? Where I had failed you? How this could be happening to me? I was doing the best for you, but you had your own agenda. I have long since forgiven you for that dreadful time.

Of course, I am now able to admit that much as I wanted to surprise you, I should have discussed my plans with you before implementing them. I suppose our children are our best teachers. But it's hard. Ask any Jewish mother.

Much love
Mom

19 May

Dearest Rebecca

An afterthought: I have come to the realisation now that in terms of what you do and how you do it, it is inevitable that you would always feel obliged to start from the bottom. You, who have never paused to consider an easy option, always refused a hand-up. Your friends and colleagues may have respected you for it; I felt you were being stubborn in your martyrdom. Those first years back in South Africa need not have been such a hardship for you. I mean, Nelson Mandela was released from prison in 1990 soon after you came home and things were changing. But you were determined to live in a suburb that was a melting pot of cultures and colours, and to rent studio space in a dilapidated degenerate warehouse in a dangerous part of downtown Johannesburg that promised to be the new cultural precinct of the city. No wonder that when you finally opened the studio after doing basic repair work and having lights and water connected, it immediately attracted down-and-out alcoholic artists who had an abundance of talent but empty pockets. I have no idea how you managed to get funding and move the studio to Venda, which is now becoming a centre where artists can live and work. Of course I am not going to mention the sleepless nights and heartache your project is giving me.

How ironic, though, that your grandfather, a Lithuanian immigrant, started his business in almost the same area as where you chose to establish your studio. He began by selling goods from a horse and cart. He had little choice since he started out with nothing. It was his determination, his indomitable spirit of adventure and will to succeed that channelled his energy and intellect into learning the language and the culture of the people, black and white, and forging a career for himself from dreams that he made come true. He also had a social conscience and was appalled at the inequality and injustice that prevailed in our society. During the time he was establishing himself in business, he committed himself to exposing the hardship, the lack of adequate housing, education and hospitalisation, in the black communities. Although he spoke Yiddish to his friends and fellow Lithuanians, his preferred language became English. He was a vociferous reader, prolific writer and articulate public speaker for the Labour Party, which subsequently led to his election as a provincial councillor – one of the few platforms where he could voice his abhorrence of the apartheid government and work for the upliftment of the disenfranchised.

Who knows, perhaps through your art, teaching and outreach projects you are continuing the work he started.

Much love
Mom

21 May

My dearest Rachel

Your involvement with psychotherapy must stop. Whenever I try
to phone you, I'm told you are attending group sessions for yourself or facilitating group workshops for others. I'm sure this is not
good for you. There are many things in life that are better left
alone. Surely one doesn't need to uncover all one's inner feelings
and emotions in order to be happy. I think it has the opposite
effect. It makes one feel dreadful about one's behaviour and terribly guilty about things you should have done or did not do. One
cannot spend years searching for an incident in one's childhood to
unravel the secrets of why you are afraid of heights, why your
mother suffocates in crowds or why your sister bites her nails.

I have this strong suspicion that you are secretly hoping to discuss
my case in your various groups. You might really enjoy exposing
all our mother–daughter stuff – the Melanie Klein nonsense of
other–mother bonding in infancy, the good and bad breast which
is supposed to explain all kinds of behaviour. Or, you may choose
an aspect of my life to present to your Freudian dream group to
throw some light on my decision to give up all the comforts of
married life and live alone. I shudder to think what your colleagues would conclude. No doubt they would find some hidden
and repressed motive from a childhood trauma. Well, Rachel, let

me assure you, there are no undisclosed or fascinating secrets to unravel. My case would not be interesting enough for your group. Moreover, I cannot imagine that your professional ethics would allow you to discuss family members, especially your Jewish mother, in your sessions. Tell me I'm right!

However, I am saddened by Eli's reaction to the divorce. He has always been like a son to us, so I can understand his difficulties in accepting the break-up, as he truly believed that we were in a life-long marriage. We were role models upholding the values, consistency and commitment of marriage. It is strange that philosophically Eli accepted his own parents' divorce some time ago, yet he upheld his parents-in-law as the shining example of how a good marriage can overcome all adversity. Perhaps for him alone we should have stayed together! He continually asks how he can explain to his children why they have four sets of grandparents and none of them live together. I wish I had some answers. I would like to find a way to placate his suppressed anger at me and remove the hurt I see in his eyes.

And anger is an emotion I have had to deal with all my life. Until recently I did not know that anger can be a positive and useful tool for bringing about change. I was conditioned to believe that my anger was a manifestation of my 'bad' character, that losing my temper was dysfunctional behaviour – that I was out of control, causing embarrassment to my husband and shame to my children and family, and eliciting pity from friends and acquaintances. In those angry years, no one pointed out to me that there were other ways of understanding anger – acknowledging that it overwhelms many women in emotionally abusive situations. You recommended Harriet G. Lerner's book *The Dance of Anger*, in which she explains that anger is a signal that our rights are being violated, our needs not being met, our beliefs, values, desires and ambitions being compromised in our relationships. She says, 'Our anger may be a signal that we are doing more and giving more than we can comfortably do or give at the expense of our own growth.' And yet women who express anger, particularly with men, are condemned, shunned and dismissed as irrational.

Do you remember a few years ago when you suggested I attend a Life Skills weekend to learn how to cope with my anger and the stress in my daily life, and to turn it into something positive? The timing was brilliant as I was at the crossroads of my life, unsure of which way to go. I did not know then whether I could gather enough courage and resolve to go through with my divorce. I was trying to reclaim my life after a near-death experience with major heart surgery.

That weekend revealed to me that there were other people like me who, while seeming to be successful, were not able to deal with the stresses and vicissitudes of their daily lives. Most of the partici-pants felt they were not getting adequate support from their part-ners in their relationships. This experience changed my life. During one of the sessions, I found myself standing in front of the group, talking to people I had never seen before and telling them about my life, my dilemma and my anger. It was scary, exposing myself to strangers. I was questioned and led into discussions with the trainer and the group. There were people out there who were listening to me – a most unusual occurrence. I was asked whether I had resentments, and then found, to my astonishment, that I had a long list of them which I thought were deeply buried and safely hidden, even from myself. I discovered not only the causes of my chronic anger but the results of it as well.

For the first time I acknowledged that I was not able to deal with my feelings of being so alone in my marriage. I suppose I should have noticed that the writing was on the wall after you all left home. I believed that I was dealing with Leah and her family's immigration to Australia, Sarah's immigration to England, the absence of grandchildren, the difficulties of Rebecca's life in America, the traumatic move from our family home, my mother's recent death and Rachel's near-fatal car accident. I had always coped with difficulties in the past, and so I was convinced that my stoicism and humour were getting me through these as well. I did not realise that I was avoiding the real issues. My denial of what was happening in my own life hardly prepared me for the onset of severe angina, mistaken diagnoses, heart failure, and subsequent emergency heart surgery to save my life. It was only when I was confronted with the possibility of dying that I encountered my own vulnerability and helplessness. My life was no longer in my control – I had to ask G-d for help if I was to survive. Only much later, a year or so, did I finally understand that my recovery was slow and lengthy not only because of the physical complications I suffered but also because of my emotional wounds and my loss of faith. My body would not heal because my feelings were so fragmented. The near-death experience forced me to confront myself.

Before the surgery and during the months of my illness, the doctors were convinced that my heart condition was caused by an uncommon disease that would disappear with time. While they were aware that there was a genetic weakness of coronary artery disease – both my father and mother had died of heart failure – the medical practitioners involved themselves with the unusual symptoms of my case. No one, including myself, was listening to the warning screams of my body unable to deal with the emotional distress. Only after the bypass surgery and during the long journey to recovery did a stranger point out to me that I had suffered from a broken heart. The assault to my body, mind and spirit changed me forever. I learned how to tune into my body and care for it, to reclaim my mind, and to seek for and return to my spirituality.

In the group session of that Life Skills weekend we were encouraged to look at ourselves. In one of the sessions we were even given mirrors to help the process. I hate looking at myself in a mirror and only do so when blow-drying my hair, putting on make-up or checking to see whether my clothes are on straight. Forced to look at my reflection, I saw myself as an ageing woman with lines around her eyes and furrows on her forehead. My hair was showing grey at the roots and needed to be coloured again. My eyes were dull and had lost their sparkle. I suddenly realised that because I had lost control of my life, I was not taking responsibility for my own unhappiness and depended on others for my well-being. I was blaming everyone else – particularly Marvin, whom I perceived as 'not being there for me'. I had been accumulating resentments against him and his family for years because I foolishly believed they should be different. I had been in denial for so long that I had lost sight of the truth. My focus was out there and not within.

But all these revelations were too serious to contemplate in a room filled with strange people trying to find themselves. As I looked around at the other participants, expecting to witness proof of their enlightenment, I burst into nervous laughter. The scene was bizarre. One woman was kissing her image, another was sobbing into her blurred reflection, a young man was glaring angrily at the face staring at him, another was hitting the mirror with his fists, a middle-aged man was smiling contentedly at his features, a young woman was plucking her eyebrows while her partner was sitting on his mirror, disgusted with the whole process. The exercise was obviously working, but I had to excuse myself and leave the room.

I know what you will say to me now. I have contradicted myself about the advantages of group therapy. I admit it has its place. The experience was incredibly informative for me. But I took what I needed from it and certainly don't want to continue ad infinitum as you seem to be doing. You have to put aside all that psychological stuff and concentrate on living in the now. You are about to have a baby. That is all you need to be thinking about.

Much love
Mom

24 May

My darling Sarah

You ask me why I did not get some help when I felt my relation-ship with your father was falling apart. Had I known how simple it was, of course I would have done so.

There were shelves of books dealing with the problems I was experiencing, such as my lack of self-esteem and my fear of facing my feelings. I was not alone. Recently, I learnt, to my great sur-prise, that most people in the Western world suffer from wounded feelings without even being aware of it – a paradoxical idea that Robert A. Johnson, a Jungian analyst, explains in the opening pages of his delightful book *The Fisher King and the Handless Maiden*: 'It is very dangerous when a wound is so common in a culture that hardly anyone knows there is a problem. There is gen-eral discontent with our way of life but almost no one knows where it comes from. One simply loses one's feeling function – the one that makes us human. And feeling we can define as the capac-ity to value or give worth to something.'

Imagine coming up with that notion from analysing two medieval tales! It is such a basic but profound idea – when people have a good feeling about you, you feel valuable in their presence. It is an indictment of our English language that we have such a poor vocabulary for describing feelings – we only have one word for love, whereas Sanskrit has ninety-six words and ancient Persian eighty. Imagine if we had at least a few dozen words for love and feelings how much richer we'd be and how much more intelligently we would behave.

I blush when I think of your growing-up years at home. You once asked me whether I was aware of the effect on you children of the arguments that took place late at night between your father and me. Most of the time I hoped or pretended that you were all asleep and oblivious to the constant bickering, harsh words, screams of rage and my tears of frustration. I suppose it must have been particularly traumatic for you, the third child, to hear your parents fighting, never quite knowing what it was about, because it all seemed to blow over by the morning, when your daily routine resumed. I refused to recognise our quarrelling as a serious problem and doubled up on my efforts to make our home as normal and happy as possible. I would never acknowledge that my role as perfect wife and mother was being compromised by a few squabbles.

My credentials as a homemaker and impeccable hostess were well established. We were always entertaining our families and friends, and your father's business acquaintances. You and your sisters were our greatest assets at our parties, for no sooner had our guests arrived than our well-trained daughters welcomed them and took their orders for drinks, then graciously served them. Not only did you help prepare the snacks and other food, you waited upon the guests, ran errands for us and were generally indispensable until it was time for you to go to bed. Why did you wait for so many years before you staged your mini-revolution? Why did you allow us to exploit you so shamelessly? You were all so accepting when you were young. We even thought you enjoyed waitressing! The rebellion came in your late teens – your fierce fight for independence and freedom. You all knew that you didn't want to perpetuate the socially frenetic way of life so sought after by suburban trendsetters – your parents and their acquaintances. And miraculously you all managed to transcend it, and have found the strength and courage to live your lives according to your own inner values and beliefs.

I often wonder how my daughters coped with my anger. I wonder, too, how they were expressing theirs. A favourite tendency of daughters is to blame their mother for all the ills that befall them. I remember a time when I found the courage to blame my mother for a multitude of things. I had realised that the sky was not going to fall in if I charged her with having hurt me, making me angry and failing to meet my needs. A mother is a great scapegoat – she is usually present, often available and always loaded with guilt feelings. I'm sure Jewish mothers carry more guilt than most other kinds of mothers. They suffer more and constantly see themselves as martyrs. (Or are these truisms with which we console ourselves?)

But I like to believe that my relationship with you and your sisters is growing stronger. Each one of us is learning to respect our differences and take responsibility for our own lives.

And one thing is for sure: writing to my daughters is my therapy.

Much love
Mom

30 May

Darling Leah

Today would have been your grandmother's birthday, always a special day in our lives. I can't help wondering what she would have thought about my divorce. I suppose I will never know whether I delayed it all these years because she would have made it too uncomfortable for me. Did I take this momentous step because she was no longer around peering over my shoulder and scolding me when I did something of which she didn't approve? You knew her best, what do you think? What is indisputable is that her story-book love affair with your grandfather was a hard act for me to follow.

Had she still been alive she would have been ninety, but longevity was not a strong suit in her family. Her poor father died at forty-five from hard work and a heart attack – it's no wonder, with very little money and a wife and ten hungry children to feed. I would like to know how these Lithuanian immigrants managed in those days, living in small rural towns without knowing the language or culture of the people, eking out a living in a trading store and bringing up their families with the right values – knowing that they had everything they needed. Can you imagine this kind of scenario today? We are forever buying things for our children, overcompensating for the violence, the abuse and lack of values in our society. And the more we give, the more we are expected to give.

My grandmother Leah scrubbed, cleaned, cooked and sewed, for her eight daughters and two sons, who all grew up believing they had a privileged upbringing and were living in a castle. She was the local medical specialist who treated broken limbs, whooping cough and infectious diseases with her home-grown remedies, habitual superstitions and traditional good sense. She grew spinach, potatoes and pumpkin on which she force-fed her children and neighbours. But it was her fame as a baker of cinnamon *bulkelach* that spread throughout the district. The story goes that the reason she made them at four a.m. when the household was asleep was that she did not want to reveal her secret ingredient. A more likely explanation is that it was only at four a.m. that she found time to bake. Yet, even though she passed on her baking skills and recipes to all her daughters, except my mother, they always complained that their *bulkelach* never tasted like hers. They spent their baking lives trying to discover her secret. (Perhaps in those days they tasted better because the children were hungry.) My mother, on the other hand, escaped to the big city to live with her grandfather and never experienced their frustration, as she had found work as a cashier in a large store. My father fell in love with her and, as they say, the rest is history.

How many fathers today insist on their children calling them by their first names? In fact, he insisted on everyone calling him Mendel – people who worked for him, people he had just met, young children and even those from different cultures who found the informality disrespectful. But they need not have worried, because everyone respected him. But he was a *luftmensch* (a Yiddish expression one can't translate – his head was in the sky), a dreamer, an idealist, a socialist, a man before his time. He always boasted that he chose the perfect wife for himself because he did not have to deal with mundane activities, like putting on two socks of the same colour or a matching pair of black shoes. There were times when your Granny Esther refused to put out his clothes for work, but she would always receive a call from his office to say that Mendel was inappropriately dressed and likely to cause embarrassment. On several occasions she had to go to the city with a discreet brown paper bag with the missing or properly matched items of clothing. There were compensations galore because when Mendel married my mother he rescued her from becoming a stereotypical Jewish housewife. She immediately forgot how to cook, sew and do domestic chores. Instead, my father had taught her how to dream, to think and to be a *mensch* – she discovered she had the potential for another way of living. He was her teacher and mentor, even instructing her in how to read and write Yiddish so that she could absorb the essence of the Yiddish poets, writers and artists who gravitated to their home. She learnt to paint, to play the piano and to sing. She was bold and had guts. She dressed in black with wildly fashionable hats and accessories. She even went for public-speaking lessons and became an innovative community leader.

It was often embarrassing for my sister and I to have parents who were different from those of our friends. Our house was too modern and avant-garde, our parents' friends were theatrical and eccentric, their political activities were unpopular. We often had crazy artists staying in our house, occupying our space and using our dining room as an art studio, while we were swept under the carpet in case we disturbed their creative output. Often we were persuaded to go out with our parents and their friends to interminable political meetings in dreary and draughty halls or to lectures in

Yiddish on Russian literature or Polish poetry. We counted ourselves lucky when, for birthday treats, we were taken to the opera, ballet or theatre. I wonder how we survived our childhood. I promised myself then that if I ever had children I would never bring them up in that way. Apart from a few lapses, I haven't, have I?

But back to the romantic love story of my parents. I am not saying their marriage was a bed of roses without thorns. There were plenty of arguments and disagreements, temper tantrums and tears, but they passed quickly and no one ever remembered what they were about. It's a great shame that Mendel's physical capabilities were not equal to his intellectual capacity. His body let him down – more specifically, his cardiovascular system. He was a semi-invalid for the last dozen years of his life which, while painful for him, was also a triumph of his indomitable spirit and an opportunity for my mother to demonstrate her exceptional 'Florence Nightingale' talents to make my father's life as pleasant and comfortable as possible.

It was only after her death that I found, stored in a concealed cupboard, a box of letters sorted in bundles tied with pink and red ribbons – love letters between my parents written from the time of their marriage until my father's death. I always knew about the existence of the letters, but it took me several years to pluck up courage to read them. It felt intrusive to pry into their private lives. I remember, particularly on birthdays and anniversaries, whenever my mother received a letter from my father she used to blush, rush upstairs and lock the door to read it in privacy. They were away from each other quite frequently, either because of my father's business trips and his political agenda or because of my mother's communal work and cultural activities which took them to various destinations. Judging from the reams of correspondence, they must have written to each other almost every day. My father's letters were romantic and ardent. He stole lines from The Song of Solomon, Shakespearean love sonnets and Yiddish folk songs. My mother was more pragmatic. She worried endlessly about his health, his diet, his overexertion and his absence from her. Her letters tended to be repetitive, even tedious at times, filled with concerns of day-to-day living. There was no earth-shattering material, only an intense correspondence between people sharing the events of their lives, but between the lines there emerged a passionate and tender love story which elevated their marriage to family legend.

Leah dear, I know you have a wonderful marriage with your Sam, and you must cherish his birthday and anniversary cards even though they are commercially printed and often consist of sayings and poems written by someone else. It's the sentiment that counts anyway! Fortunately, you will not be put in the position of finding and reading love letters when I'm no longer around. Your father did not like the written word and would never commit himself on paper. He once told me how, after he had written and signed certain documents in business dealings he had with some unsavoury character, they were used in evidence against him. He swore after that experience that he would never, without due care, put pen to paper again. His favourite saying was 'Make a mistake but keep the receipt.' I, on the other hand, used to write long letters to him, particularly after we had quarrelled. I could always express myself better on paper than in person. It was as though the floodgates opened when I began to write and I wrote many letters into the early hours of the morning expressing how I felt about things, discussing our relationship, explaining why I was angry and saying how I wish our relationship would change. He did something quite strange with my letters. He kept them and filed them, rarely commenting on receiving them but waiting until another quarrel inevitably erupted. With a grand flourish, he then flashed the offending letter in my face and read me sections of it. The context, time and place seemed unimportant to him – only that I had committed myself to paper and provided him with the written proof of what I had said, often in anger and sadness. It took me several years to learn the lesson and refrain from writing any more letters.

I missed the letter-writing. I missed the communication I thought was taking place. I missed seeing my words on paper. I missed sharing my thoughts, feelings, anger and love with my husband. I had discovered that letter-writing needs a reader who wants to read and will listen to the words. As Annie Dillard says in *The Writing Life*:

> The written word is weak. Many people prefer life to it.
> Life gets your blood going, and it smells good. Writing is
> mere writing, literature is mere [literature]. It appeals
> only to the subtlest senses – the imagination's vision –
> and the moral sense, and the intellect. This writing that
> you do, that so thrills you, that so rocks and exhilarates
> you, as if you were dancing next to the band, is barely
> audible to anyone else. The reader's ear must adjust
> down from loud life to the subtle, imaginary sounds of
> the written word. An ordinary reader picking up a book
> can't hear a thing; it will take half an hour to pick up the
> writing's modulations, its ups and downs and louds and
> softs.

Ah well, that was a long time ago. And now almost thirty years later I'm writing e-mail letters to my daughters in cyberspace. And what can be better fun than that? They can delete what I say by pressing a key or save it in a file called Mom. The letters don't need to be tied up with pink or red ribbons and kept for posterity. We are living in a throw-away era, which has its merits, especially for people like me who tend to keep everything. But now that is changing. I need to throw away things I have accumulated. I need some space. Nor am I prepared to allow the memorabilia of your childhood, school-years and university days to continue cluttering my cupboards. Either reclaim your stuff or I'll throw it away. I am going to live in the now and not in the past.

Much love
Mom

10 June

Darling Leah

I'm pleased you were taking notice when I said I am throwing away all the clutter in my house. I will certainly arrange to give the toys, books, photographs, desk and that old rocking horse to Max to put in his container when he immigrates to Perth next month. I must say that I'm surprised and disappointed in him. I cannot understand why he is leaving South Africa – he has a fantastic business, a beautiful house, masses of friends and family, and a great future here. What is he going to do in Perth? He will struggle to make a living and maintain a decent lifestyle. He should go to a shrink. He needs to change his attitude and stop being so gloomy about the future. Why can't he be positive and see the good in the country? Is he so ignorant and prejudiced that he cannot acknowledge that black empowerment doesn't mean the end for bright young white entrepreneurs? Unfortunately, his fears will follow him wherever he goes.

No, I don't intend throwing out our family's recipes for *babka*, *bulkelach*, borscht, sweet-and-sour cabbage soup, *kishka*, *cholent* and those other dishes you mentioned, which I can't be bothered to make any more. I have kept them safely in a large cardboard box and you are quite welcome to them. In fact, I may pack them into a suitcase and bring them as unaccompanied baggage when I come for the Batmitzvah. You are the only one of my daughters who might find them useful. The others are too busy with their careers to spend time in their kitchens. But you will have to sort them out, as there are literally hundreds. I hadn't realised that in the last few years your grandmother became an addictive compulsive collector of recipes. She found them in the strangest places – dentists' and doctors' waiting rooms, hairdressers, restaurants, various upmarket offices and even hotels where she extracted them from books, magazines or newspapers. She persuaded her friends and acquaintances to part with their favourite recipes, which she compiled into a rough book. I must say she acknowledged where each one came from and graded many of them as excellent, very good, good and poor. So, when you see 'Etty's stuffed gefilte fish with kumquats' with a *v.g.* and a star, you will know it's the real thing. However, do not trust the recipes she managed to extract from the chefs at the Hilton Hotel, the Colony or those overpriced restaurants, because you can be sure that they never declared all the ingredients and they certainly would not enlighten her by divulging their methods.

No, my darling Leah, I am not prepared to sit at my desk in front of the computer and type out all my favourite recipes for you. I have better things to do with my time. Also, it irritates me a little when you ask me, for example, for my recipe for *kneidlach* and then you treble the quantities and tell me they were either rock hard or had disintegrated. I distinctly told you to use the recipe exactly as I gave it to you – if you have to make three batches, so be it. The maximum number of eggs you can use at a time for *kneidlach* (and my hot-mild sponge cake) is six, with six tablespoons of schmaltz (not oil) and six tablespoons of iced water (not water at room temperature). The secret ingredient, of course, is the tablespoon of ground almonds. You must not beat the mixture too much and must use a wooden spoon to keep it light. This recipe has never failed me, and whoever has eaten my *kneidlach* always remembers the texture and taste. I do not object to giving you recipes, remedies and advice, but please follow them.

I am wondering whether the book I sent you by Laura Esquivel, *Like Water for Chocolate*, has anything to do with your compulsion to cook in such large quantities. The book is, of course, quite marvellous. The author weaves traditional Spanish recipes into the love stories of her characters and shows how their lives are influenced by the kind of exotic dishes Mama Elena prepares for special occasions. I love her recipe for Chabela's wedding cake – 175 grams refined granulated sugar, 300 grams cake flour sifted three times, 17 eggs, grated peel of one lime – which has to be multiplied by ten for Pedro and Rosaura's wedding, since 'they were preparing a cake not for eighteen people but for 180'. How unfortunate that, after she had prepared the filling and the fondant icing, and inadvertently mixed them with tears of sadness, the guests were overcome with a strange intoxication that scattered them on the patio, where they vomited collectively, an omen of the ill-fated marriage and lost love that unfolds in the pages of the novel. No matter how many dishes Mama Elena prepares to heal the wounds of the loveless marriage, even attempting quail in rose petal sauce, and turkey mole with almonds and sesame seeds, the tragic consequences cannot be evaded. So be warned, Leah! Only cook when you are in the right mood. Sometimes, the way to a man's heart is not through his stomach.

And I can vouch for that. Throughout my marriage I spent a great deal of time in the kitchen preparing dishes I thought would please your father. I was always trying out new recipes, concocting delectable dishes and going to cookery demonstrations. I was even taught by an illustrious chef how to prepare traditional Chinese food. I learnt to make all kinds of Jewish dishes from my aunts and my grandmother. We entertained a great deal and our guests loved coming for meals and parties, never knowing whether I would be serving French, Italian or Portuguese cuisine, Swiss fondue or Thai curry. It took me more years than I care to admit to realise that my husband cared nothing for my cooking. He only asked me what food we were preparing so that he could match it up with a suitable wine. After our dinners he used to tell me how much the guests enjoyed the particular wine he served and the cognac or port that followed the meal.

I took particular care to make Shabbat dinners special in our house, but Marvin always picked at his food, complaining that the beef was too well done, the chicken not crisp enough, the lamb overcooked and the roast potatoes not the way he liked them. I took his criticism personally, but there were other reasons why he was rarely hungry at dinnertime. Most weekdays he took business colleagues to lunch, entertained bank managers at fashionable restaurants and met his fishing buddies, golfing friends or bridge or poker crowd for lunch. At one o'clock on Fridays, a table at a favourite restaurant was always booked in his name. He took pride in the fact that all his business deals were struck over good food and a bottle of vintage wine, never in an office behind a desk. After all that wining and dining, he had little appetite when he came home in the evening.

Why is it that we are forever discussing food? Aren't there other subjects that are more interesting? It's quite strange how hung up people are about what they eat. They either discuss a new diet they will begin on Monday, giving many excuses why the previous one didn't work, or they pontificate on the nutritious value of certain foods and the harmful effects of others. All their information comes from American research written up in a variety of popular magazines. I am always poorly informed about these subjects because I never get to read magazines. Nonetheless, one of my friendships is exclusively food oriented. Whenever I receive a call from Sonia Cohen, which is usually twice a week, we discuss food: which supermarket has specials, the spiralling cost of kosher meat, the prohibitive price of fish, and the best fruit and vegetable shops. No matter how we start a conversation – a bit of gossip about a mutual friend – we always finish up with what she is about to serve her family for dinner. Is this a Jewish thing? Or is it an occupational hazard of wives and mothers? I am quite fond of Sonia, but the telephone calls are boring and time-consuming. She is not an adventurous cook, so her menus tend to be the same even when she wants to excel for her bridge-party luncheons or impress overseas visitors with her five-course dinners. Her presentation and preparation of the food is so predictable. But her husband and family think she is the best Jewish cook around. So who am I to criticise?

But I'm at it again.

Much love
Mom

17 June

Leah darling

I'm so glad you agree that there are more important things to life. No more talk of food. Yes, I do want to discuss with you what you are going to wear for the Batmitzvah.

I am hoping Sam will go out and buy you a new outfit. He has exquisite taste, and whenever he wants you to look stunning, he goes off, without you, on a shopping spree to his favourite designer shop and comes back with beautiful garments. His explanation to me makes perfect sense: 'Leah is always shopping for the household and for the children – their clothes, shoes, underwear, soccer boots, and ballet shoes – so when she shops for herself she is always in a hurry and goes to K Mart or the bargain basements.' I'm sure Sam is grateful that you spend so little on yourself, but with your habit of looking at the price first, before the colour and style, you are bound to buy clothes that are cheap and nasty. So leave it to Sam – he has great taste. He used to love the clothes you wore before you immigrated down under. But then, your grandmother and I always went shopping with you at those fashionable boutiques. With your petite figure, long hair and good looks you were a pleasure to dress. You were the only one of my four daughters who took an interest in what you wore. It was probably your grandmother's flair and passion for style that sparked your interest. Yes, I know things have changed – you are a mother of six and have to dress modestly, with sleeves up to your elbows, skirts below your knees and high necklines. But it's not written in the *Chumash* that the colours and style have to be so drab and shapeless.

I wish I had kept the dramatic clothes, hats and jewellery your grandmother wore with such confidence. But what would I have done with them? I would never have had the guts to wear those outfits, even if there was an extravagant occasion that might call for them. Her kind of life was ideal for showing off her clothes – she was always attending meetings, conferences, gala occasions, fund-raising functions or travelling somewhere, here or overseas. No wonder *Lady Fair* magazine once voted her one of the ten best-dressed women. I mean, the irony of it: growing up in Amersdorp, a little backwater town with a handful of Jewish families, where she and her sisters cut out newspaper patterns and made their dresses from rolls of calico their father managed to procure from travelling salesmen. While her sisters always spoke with pride of how they managed to clothe their large family, explaining in detail how they made their own bras and petticoats from the offcuts, my mother kept silent as though she had never worn those white hand-sewn country clothes of her childhood and adolescence. It's strange that while her sisters were excellent needlewomen I never remember seeing my mother in our home with a needle and thread. It was as though her life began at eighteen when she came to live in Johannesburg.

There are so many questions I wish I would have asked her about her life. I took for granted most things she did because of her amazing energy and capacity for work. She seemed to manage everything – whether it was organising enormous charity functions, mediating between quarrelling family members, getting dressed to the nines to address conferences or fund-raisers, working tirelessly in her garden, or just being there for those of us who needed her support. I wish my attitude to her motley collection of friends had been more tolerant: Lawrence, the dress designer, who adored making stylish outfits for her; André, the frustrated jeweller, who depended on her willingness to wear his creations; Mr Hochenstadt, the gardner, whom she encouraged to experiment with his ideas of colour-coded planting; Irene Stollen, the artist, who painted seven portraits of her, never satisfied she had captured her essence; and Olga, who loved concocting exotic dishes for her to taste before including them in a glossy cookbook.

I wonder if she knew that I felt privileged being her daughter.

Much love
Mom

23 June

Rachel and Eli, my dearest children

I breathe again. And I need to put my feelings down in writing.

Witnessing the birth of your baby was the most memorable experience of my life. I am in awe of the miracle of birth. The physical process that transforms a foetus into a perfect human being with spiritual, emotional and instinctive needs is the most beautiful and unforgettable thing in this world. The life-force of the mother's energy pushing this tiny, strong, squirming, breathing baby out into the world is an extraordinary phenomenon for a grandmother to see and the greatest gift a daughter can give a mother. I felt as though I were taking part in one of the wonders of the universe, as if G-d were letting us into His secret of creation. In fact, the combination of husband–wife love, sister love, and mother–daughter love created an aura in your bedroom so powerful that I felt humbled. I am privileged and will be forever grateful that you allowed me to be part of the event. I cannot thank you enough for overriding my wishes and choosing a home birth under the guidance of those splendidly competent and caring midwives. They provided us with all the support, confidence and courage we needed through the labour. What wonderful women they are!

As for the baby you gave birth to – she is precious! In fact, she is the most beautiful baby I have ever seen – apart from my own. I think she looks a lot like me, although Eli seems to think that she has the features of his family. As they are good-looking, I really don't mind at this stage. Let him think what he likes. No doubt his parents will agree that she looks exactly the way he did when he was born. Obviously time will tell. Newborn babies seem to take on the appearance of whoever is looking at them. She also looks exceptionally intelligent, which is a genetic trait for which our family happens to be renowned. I also noticed that she has a will of her own – shown particularly when she latched on to your breast – and that kind of determination and purpose in life is a quality that you and your sisters have inherited from your grand-parents and great-grandparents. When I held her soon after she was born, I felt a surge of joy such as I have never experienced before. With her little face nestling in my neck, I whispered to her to forgive me for wanting her to be born in a hospital. I am sure that is the moment we bonded. She looked at me through her squinting, unfocused eyes and seemed to accept my apology.

I mean, come to think of it, a home birth is the most civilised and sensible way to have a baby. These poor unfortunate mothers and fathers who are socially conditioned to go for the hospital option of clinical coldness do not know what they are missing. I feel sorry for them. I feel sorry for all women in maternity wards all over the world. I feel sorry that I have only now discovered how babies are born. I intend to start an action group for mothers to encourage their daughters and sons-in-law to have their babies in their beds. I will campaign tirelessly for this experience that has changed my life so dramatically.

Have I told you how much I approve of the colour you painted the baby's room? When the initial shock wore off, I realised that it was because I had never seen a baby's room, in fact, any room, painted that original and unusual shade of orange, which is now a fashion colour called pumpkin. The way you have colour-coordinated the room with those bold reds, blues and yellows of the curtains is making a real statement. I have always maintained that all colours go together and this is a perfect example. The exception, of course, is the turquoise-blue dresser with the orange knobs, which I'm confident will fade with time and use, but otherwise I suggest giving it a coat of white paint – an interesting contrast. It is quite coincidental that when I was shopping for the baby a few days ago I saw the most stunning outfit for myself in a shade of pumpkin. As soon as I put it on I felt calm and centred. It had an astonishing impact on my psyche and I was able to feel the energy and feminine presence of Mother Earth. My new granddaughter in her pumpkin palace, surrounded by love, warmth and positive energy, will no doubt grow into someone who will bring joy to the world.

Now that you have a daughter of your own, you will understand that special relationship that exists between mothers and daughters. I know you will be promising yourself to make none of the mistakes that I made with you. Well, it's certainly worth a try. I am not convinced that the mistakes are avoidable. I understand that you are feeling very fragile and vulnerable after the birth of little Indi. It's really a nice name when you get used to it. A bit strange, but quite nice. I suppose one doesn't need to name a baby girl after a flower – a country is, after all, more important. I suppose with all your yoga exercises and your Eastern method of breath control during labour, the name should not be such a surprise. Thankfully, she will be given a Hebrew name in synagogue which will also be her second name – Indi Batsheva. Unusual, but a politically correct combination.

I will respect your wishes to give you, Eli and little Gideon time to yourselves to bond with the baby over the next couple of weeks. I think it commendable that Eli has taken paternity leave, though, quite frankly, when you have your mother living so nearby, I don't really see the necessity. However, under the circumstances I will not obtrude on your arrangements. But I hope your pride will not prevent you from asking for my help. After all, when Leah had her babies she was not ashamed to admit that she could not have managed without my help. I always bathed them and they seldom cried. As a result all the children love water to this day. I know how to pacify babies when they cry, and exactly when it is time for their feed, when it is time to change their nappies and when it is time to put them to sleep. A grandmother knows these things instinctively. But if you want to be obstinate and independent, so be it. It is only my opinion, of course, but we who care about you would all agree that you need to regain your health and strength after the stressful and exhausting labour you endured. While the birth was a wonderful experience for us, the spectators, it was something of a major trauma for you. We learnt afterwards that you had second thoughts about having an audience and refusing painkilling drugs. You even admitted to us that had you known the length of the labour and its intensity, you may have opted for an elective epidural Caesarean.

I know you could not have been serious when you said that, because you have told me many times that it was a 'cop-out' for me to have had my last two children by Caesarean section. No clinical explanations or medical reasons ever satisfied you. No evidence of previous difficulties and anatomical abnormalities was acceptable to you. You believe even now that it was an unforgivable and cowardly act to forgo the bonding experience of natural childbirth for the advantages of a sterile delivery in an operating theatre. You have never forgiven me. Moreover, you imply that all the disagreements we have ever had stem from our lack of bonding at the moment of your birth. It seems that one of your psycho-analytic gurus put this notion into your head, and that it has influenced your thinking and impaired your vision, which otherwise is quite clear. As a result you are now punishing me by withholding your baby from my expert care.

I cannot help remembering that when I held you in my arms for the first time I was overcome with such intense feelings of happiness that I sobbed uncontrollably. The doctor and nursing staff came to comfort me, telling me it was perfectly natural to feel depressed, especially as the baby was another girl. Imagine that! Imagine that anyone who had three daughters would want a boy. You were perfect. You were what I wanted. What would your sisters, your father and I have done with a boy? We did not know anything about boys. The only person I know who wanted me to have a son was my mother-in-law, and I certainly did not want to give her that satisfaction. Each year I rejoice and celebrate the miracle of your birth, but never more so than on your seventeenth birthday when, again sobbing uncontrollably with joy, I thanked G-d that your life had been spared after your car accident. In spite of your injuries, the spirit within you shone brightly. It was the end of your adolescence and the beginning of your new life as an extraordinary woman.

Much love
Mom

27 June

My darling Rebecca

The birth of your new god-daughter, Indi Batsheva, seems to have had the same profound effect on you as it did on me. I am so happy we were able to share this incredible experience. I still cannot describe my feelings. It transcends everything I have witnessed in my life. I know that I will be eternally grateful to Rachel and Eli for sharing the precious gift of their daughter's birth with us.

I am convinced that it has shifted your way of thinking. I feel more confident now to raise the subject again. But, being a typical Jewish mother, I could not keep myself from wishing that, having witnessed the birth of your sister's baby, you would have decided to have one of your own! I know that I've promised not to mention it again, but I really can't resist. You would make a perfect mother. You love children and they adore you. As I've repeatedly told you, I have no problem with you bringing up a child as a single parent. Of course, it would have been simpler had you married that nice Jewish architect who was so crazy about you, but I am happy that you have a loving partner, who is like a daughter to me, and that your household is warm, strong, caring and joyous. A perfect environment for a child. You could even have a home birth! I'm sold on the idea. Not that I am being pushy or prescriptive, but you could reconsider your decision, and give meaning to the causes to which I would like to devote my time.

Apart from launching a support group for divorced mothers who have children scattered in the Diaspora, I want to promote home births among middle-class families. This would immeasurably improve family dynamics and promote 'bonding'. (That awful jargon word but a worthwhile concept, unlike 'quality time', which is used as a poor excuse when you see your children only seldom but strive to have a good time when you're together. I mean, if we had *quantity* time with our children and grandchildren, we could avoid a lot of stress, angst and guilt.) Furthermore, I would advocate, in certain cases, the desirability of same-sex households as an ideal environment in which to nurture and raise babies. The child would have a privileged upbringing from two committed women who intrinsically possess qualities of wisdom, compassion and caring. In your case, all you would need to do is find time from your busy schedule, choose a suitable donor, persuade your partner to give up her independence, find a way to make a lucrative living, move into an appropriate home near good schools and attend to a few other practical details which I'm sure you can work out. It will certainly make me happy to be your child's grandmother. And not only that: we, as a nuclear family, would serve as an impressive role model for my organisation.

I wish you would reconsider your options. Persuade Trish of the long-term benefits of a child in your household. Think of the pleasure and *nachas* it will give me. I will even undertake to sponsor the child's schooling. I will also persuade your father to set up a trust fund. What else do I need to do to convince you?

Much love
Mom

1 July

Dearest Rebecca

After your return from Philadelphia, we seemed to lose that strong bond that held us together while you were in exile. I suppose it was inevitable. You were re-establishing your life in South Africa, choosing to live in a suburb that was not easily accessible for a Jewish mother bringing chicken soup. I wonder whether the locale was deliberately chosen to keep me at a distance. Your busy schedule of teaching, running the studio and travelling to various outreach projects in rural areas made it extremely difficult for us to get together regularly. When we did, our conversation revolved around our daily lives – we never seemed able to talk about the real issues that kept our correspondence so alive when you were ten thousand miles away. How fortunate for me that your funders insisted that the studio acquire a computer with Internet access to connect you to the rest of the world. And they insisted that you learn how to use it. The bonus for me is that you encouraged me to continue our correspondence, even though it's mostly one-sided. So, I no longer have to be a nagging mom asking you when you are going to visit me. Nor do you have to be riddled with guilt when you don't phone me every day. I have e-mail which keeps me happy even when you don't reply.

Your unexpected invitation for a dinner party and weekend in your new home in that nice banana plantation in Venda was proof of the 'e-mail fix'. How I enjoyed being with you and your friends! Your dinner table looked splendid with the flamboyant arrangement of wild strelitzias, purple irises, prickly pears and artichoke flowers. Where did you find them? It was so reminiscent of your grandmother's flair for colour and unusual combinations. The meal was delicious, especially those exotic-tasting Thai curry dishes served in colourful handmade porcelain plates. I'm sure I need not have been concerned that you included mopani worms in your stew, even though they are considered a delicacy in your part of the world. As I have suffered no ill effects, I'm sure your ingredients were above board. What a delight to find that you are after all a closet colourist! All these years you have been stifling your attraction for the exotic.

What a relief for me that the sombreness of your art no longer impinges on your life. At last you have melded your art and life into a workable combination. Trish's influence on the way you live has been remarkable. She has made your home light, airy and colourful, with even a hint of kitsch in the decor. Your embroidered cushions and geometrically woven carpets are unique and lovely. Your collection of African wooden figures carved from twisted, gnarled and burnt-out tree trunks is rather too raw for my taste, especially as your guests kept tripping over them. But, all in all, your home looks like other people's homes. In fact, I would be quite comfortable bringing my friends to visit – though not without an invitation, of course. Apart from a few of your dark soulful Rembrandt-like etchings, the art on the walls is pleasant. You now have interesting friends who are fun. They are neither poor and destitute, nor immersed in art, politics or gender issues. Amazingly, they are ordinary people with regular jobs. A few years ago this would have been inconceivable.

After the dinner party, you remarked how much happier I am looking since my divorce. I was surprised at this observation coming from one of my daughters. I know it's a difficult balancing act you have to perform between your parents. Luckily for me, Marvin is hundreds of miles away at the coast and visits Johannesburg infrequently. In this way I am able to cope. Yes, I am certainly reclaiming my life, my beliefs, my needs, my health and my inner being. I wake up in the morning and I see the new day. I am not weighed down with a burden I cannot carry. I am feeling extraordinarily content.

Maybe I was too immature to get married when I did. Marvin was a thirty-one-year-old bachelor who had travelled the world and lived his life as he pleased. I was young and overprotected – a starry-eyed bride expecting to be the centre of her husband's affection. Until I married I had been living in the same house in which I was born. At twenty, my expectations had their roots in the romantic fairy-story notion of people getting married and living happily every after. And when I met your father, he was my knight in shining armour ready to carry me off on a wild adventure. The fascination for me then was the difference in our age, the difference in our way of life, the difference in our upbringing on different continents. Our values and interests were so diverse. The anecdotes of his childhood and adolescence in England and Europe never tired me. His accounts of his family, travels and exploits were a source of wonderment. I had never met anyone like him. I was a captive audience for Marvin's stories. I felt like Desdemona listening to the exotic tales Othello told: 'She lov'd me for the dangers I had pass'd, And I lov'd her that she did pity them.'

I was flattered that a man so much older than me, who was

worldly and wise, was interested in me, a young girl whose head was filled with dreams of saving the world. He was not only in love with me, he was determined to marry me. I was swept off my feet by the panache of his courtship. His maturity and self-confidence made the clumsy bumblings of the young denim-clad university students with whom I went to jazz concerts seem ridiculous. I was wined and dined in high style. The sophistication of the lifestyle to which he introduced me I found attractive and appealing. I felt superior to my peers and considered myself lucky to be whisked away from the youthful academic life of the campus. I was certainly not in a space where I could have listened to the warnings from my friends and family. Having been told that I was too young, too unworldly, ill-prepared for a bachelor who, having sown his wild oats, finally wanted to settle down with someone like me, I thought them envious of me. I was in love with the idea of being in love. It was enough. No marriage counsellor could have dissuaded me from embarking on my adventure into the unknown.

And I regret very little of my life. There were more good times than bad. The good times were filled with laughter, building a home for our family, watching our children grow. The bad times were my anger at things I could not change and the frustration of living with a man with whom I had so little in common. Nor had I ever learned how to deal with our differences, or how to connect with his family, friends and the things that were important to him.

Having walked away from it, I now want to do other things. I want to see the turtles on the Galápagos Islands, I want to go whale-watching off Antarctica, I want to go star-gazing in the desert, I want to meditate in the Himalayas, I want to swim in the turquoise sea of the Emerald Isles, I want to do a further degree in Jewish Studies at Oxford, I want to meet interesting scholars and explorers, I want to write a novel. All is possible.

Much love
Mom

12 July

My dearest Leah

Now that Rachel has given birth to her beautiful baby in the best possible circumstances, I am duly chastised for my doubts about a home birth. In fact, while I don't recommend it for you, if you and Sam are contemplating more children, I would be prepared to talk to your friends about the advantages and sheer joy of giving birth to a baby at home. Of course, the grandmother would have to be included in the process because her presence as a witness to this miracle of birth is essential for the success of this mind-altering experience. It would certainly be helpful for my campaign to enrol other people, particularly grandmothers, who have had this experience. We can discuss it at more length when I arrive in Perth, and perhaps you can invite several of your friends for an informal tea to discuss my project in more detail.

I now need to discuss more elevated matters with you – the spiritual aspect of the Batmitzvah. I am pleased that you are emphasizing the significance of the Batmitzvah in terms of Torah learning and insisting that Gavriela knows that the event is not simply about having a big party with great food and friends and relations dressed to the nines.

However, I feel that the theme of 'Women in the Bible' for the dinner dance is dull and dreary in the new millennium. Please don't misinterpret my words, as you often do, or presume that I don't think our biblical mothers were formidable role models for our generation. Indeed I do. Nevertheless, I feel something more upbeat would enhance the atmosphere of the dinner dance, particularly as the men and women will be required to dance separately, which always changes the dynamics of a party. Remember the speech Gavriela made in Israel, at the age of ten, for Tzippy's Batmitzvah, when she expressed her wish to have her Batmitzvah in Hollywood because she visualised herself as a movie star. I cannot imagine, even though she is now two years older, that she has changed so radically that she sees herself as Queen Esther or Ruth the Moabite, rather than Liza Minnelli, Shirley Bassey or even Madonna.

I do not wish to suggest that you compromise your strong views of what is proper, but I would like you to loosen up, particularly as your sisters and many of your friends attending are more comfortable with things familiar to them in the age in which we live. You may consider getting some advice from one of those people who professionally coordinate decor, food and music. If they are like the ones in Johannesburg, you are guaranteed a function that is over the top and will be spoken about for months after the event. I have been to a few Barmitzvahs and weddings lately and they are like Hollywood happenings.

In fact I mentioned your upcoming function to my friend Vince, who often assists one of these 'choreographic designers' (my coinage, as I don't know what they call themselves) in setting up the halls in various venues. After I had told him about your Orthodox community and the traditional value system of your family home, he came up with a lively but conservative idea for the decor. He suggested a colourful backdrop of a Hollywood boulevard gleaming with gold glitter to highlight billboards show-ing famous women movie stars who have featured in historical or biblical films over the past few decades. Flashing neon lights will pinpoint the location of the kosher hamburger and hot-dog stands for the young people, the counters with hot brisket on rye for the adults, and the salad and fresh-fruit bars for the vegetari-ans. A separate ice-cream stand with every conceivable colour and flavour of *pareve* ice creams with contrasting toppings would add to the atmosphere of the fast-food outlets in Rodeo Drive. I love his brilliant suggestion of black tablecloths with gold dust and sil-ver stars to offset the gilded polystyrene Oscars on each table – a theme that can be carried through to the printing of the invita-tions and the *benching* books containing the grace to be read after the meal. The guests, of course, can take them home after the function to remind them of Gavriela's Batmitzvah. Vince main-tains that the reduced expense of the simple meal will offset the cost of the decor. He agrees that a versatile one-person band will accommodate the Chasidic and Israeli dancing as well as the teenagers' demand for pop and rap music. Unfortunately, he did not elaborate further on his ideas, as he knew I was not going to pay him for his time and expertise. However, if you feel we can use his creativity to good effect to realise an updated version of your uninspired theme of 'Women in the Bible', let me know at once.

I won't be able to write you any more long e-mails before I leave for Perth, as there is too much to do. I need to buy presents for all the children, which is always quite a mission in terms of time and money. I also need to find a nice gift for you and Sam. And it's no use telling me that I don't need to bring presents – the children can't wait for me to open my suitcases to see what I have brought them. I will probably buy them clothes again. They always look so adorable in the things that I choose. As for me, I will probably have to wear one of my old outfits again, as I certainly won't be able to afford anything new. Being the mother and grandmother, I don't suppose anyone will notice what I wear. But I do need to attend to a number of personal things before I leave, and I don't only mean a pedicure, that special new manicure with fibreglass, my annual revitalising facial procedure, a tint and cut at Gertie's hairdresser, a leg wax and so forth. I need to organise my financial affairs and arrange for overdraft facilities with the bank. It's at times like these, when I have to buy an air ticket, renew my visa, order traveller's cheques and pay my rates, electricity and taxes out of a depleted bank account, that I miss being married to your father. He always attended to the boring practical details, particularly making finance available when I needed it. But, as your sister Rebecca keeps telling me, it's a lesson in empowerment every time I do something that I never did before.

Whenever I feel a wave of self-pity – the 'poor me' complaint – I open the pages of Rosalind Miles's *The Women's History of the World* and immediately feel better. I am reminded that it was early women, not men, who were the food gatherers and were responsible for 'child care, leatherwork, making garments, cooking, pottery, weaving grasses, fashioning beads and ornaments, construction of shelters, tool making and medicinal healing':

> From the very first, then, the role of the first women was wider, their contribution to human evolution immeasurably more significant than has ever been accepted. Dawn woman, with her mother and grandmother, her sisters and aunts, and even with a little help from her hunting man, managed to accomplish almost everything that

subsequently made 'homo' think himself 'sapiens'. There is every sign that man himself recognised this.

And so, dear Leah, the women through the ages, in every society, did it all. Why, then, do we sometimes succumb to this helpless-female syndrome?

Must rush now and prepare for my trip, the Batmitzvah and our reunion. Three major events to look forward to and my expectations are high.

I can hardly wait to see you all.

Much love
Mom

22 July

Dearest Rachel

Your announcement via e-mail has profoundly surprised me. No
wonder you did not want to tell me your plans when we were face
to face at the Shabbat table. You were right, of course. It has given
me some time to think about your impetuous decision to go to
Perth for Gavriela's Batmitzvah with Eli, Gideon, and your six-
week-old baby.

Yes, I do know that you don't have to pay for Indi's airfare, and
that you pay only half-price for Gideon, but can you afford it on
your earnings? And how are you going to travel with a tiny baby?
Is it wise to do so? The trip is long and tedious. How will you
manage with all the baby paraphernalia – nappies, blankets, clothing, creams, carrycots and all that stuff? What if she cries on the
plane and disturbs other passengers? I am trying to understand
your reasoning that it is the best time to travel with an infant –
especially because you are breastfeeding on demand and don't get
much sleep anyway.

Yes, I know you want to show off your new baby to your sisters
and their children and that you want to be with us. I also know
how you hate to miss out on anything. You hinted that you may
want to discuss the possibility, with Leah and her family, of immi-

grating to Australia. Is this a post-baby aberration, or have you been hatching this idea for a while?

Well, if you have made up your mind to come, I know I can't dissuade you. It may after all be a wonderful opportunity for a full reunion. Of course, it's a mother's greatest joy to have her children all together. Imagining my four daughters under one roof again gives me goose bumps.

As long as I don't think about the logistics of the exercise, it's a great idea. I will leave it to you and your sisters to work it all out. I promise I will try not to interfere in the arrangements. I will need my strength.

Much love
Mom

15 September

My darling daughters

After the splendid success of Gavriela's Batmitzvah, I feel I owe
you an explanation for my long silence. Only now am I able to tell
you about my feelings during our get-together in the Marapana
Wildlife Lodge. I am also pleased to tell you that I have made a
remarkable recovery from my nervous breakdown.

I need not remind you of the fun we had in the preparation of the
Holy-wood theme and how each one of us managed to come up
with novel and creative ideas for the party. The brilliant one-
person band livened up the Israeli folk dancing, as well as that
strange aerobic-type frenzy in which the men and women excelled
by dancing separately. It was flattering that the guests considered
the speeches we made to Gavriela one of the highlights of the
evening, and judging from their nods of approval and laughter
they obviously appreciated our feminist humour.

Yet, it was with a sense of relief that we finally arranged a three-
day retreat out of the city to see the kookaburras, koalas and kan-
garoos in their natural habitat at Marapana Wildlife Lodge. And,
what is more amazing, we even arranged on our last evening
together a few hours to ourselves – without husbands, partner
and children – or even the baby, who, mercifully, was in a four-

hour sleeping pattern between feeds. Our intention was to reaffirm our mother–daughter–sister relationship.

I felt emotionally warm, physically contented and mentally relaxed sitting with my daughters in front of a log fire in the rustic wooden chalet situated in the Western Australian bush. We had managed to find a space in which we felt good about ourselves – reminiscing about funny childhood episodes, awkward adolescent moments, trivial worries, humorous situations and precious times we had shared. It has always been a source of wonder to me that after so many years apart your friendship is still so strong, your understanding of each other so profound. The warmth, the laughter and companionship lulled me into a false complacency. I should have known better. I should have anticipated that, although you are so alike in appearance, so modest about your good qualities, so unassuming about your achievements, there lurks within each of you something of the wild wolf that suddenly appears out of dark hidden recesses, pouncing on unsuspecting mortals like me for the sole purpose of shocking and maddening them.

It is hardly surprising that it was you, Sarah, always delighting in the effect of the dramatic moment on your listeners, who started the avalanche of pronouncements that descended on us with such ferocity in the quiet and peaceful mountain resort. You hardly raised your voice as you said:

> As soon as we return, we will be packing up our lives in London to live in Chicago for a few years.

Waiting a few moments for the desired effect – absolute surprise and silence – you continued in a matter-of-fact tone of voice:

Cedric has been given an offer by his company to revive the office in downtown Chicago, where the rental is cheap, most of the upmarket companies having moved to the suburbs. His executive directors want him to test the American market for his ergonomic designs for the year 2004. Apparently, the Brits don't have a budget for future inventions beyond 1999.

We all had something to say at that point, but Sarah was playing it down, avoiding as best as she could the inevitable session of inter-rogation and advice:

No, I don't actually know what the designs will look like or what their function will be, except that they will be user-friendly. The only thing I know is that Cedric has been working secretly with some of the top fashion designers in Milan, so I suspect that at least some of his designs will be functional trendy clothing – the kind that has the latest technology built into the garment – small cell-phones, mini-computers, electronic diaries, Internet accessories and all that other stuff. His company reckons the Americans will love it.

No, the offer carries no guarantees but his British bosses have promised us help with the move.

No, I will probably not be able to work because with my specific qualifications – women's development in Third World countries – I probably won't find a job even if I could get a work permit.

No, I don't know how I will explain to my organisation

that I'm leaving after doing all I did to land this job. And I'm ashamed to admit that I had to stretch the truth a bit to impress them with my previous experience.

Yes, we will have to sell our house if we can, or find tenants, so that we can pay back the mortgage we owe the bank.

No, I don't imagine that we can financially recover the improvements we put into the house, nor do I believe that the potential buyer or tenant will appreciate the designs or the quality of materials we used.

No, Mom, we cannot take our steel fridge and steel gas stove to America. Nor can we take our steel shelves, copper water pipes and designer gadgets.

No, I don't have the faintest idea how we will break the news to our close circle of friends who came to London because we were there.

Yes, I will need advice on how to uproot our child from her nursery school after spending almost a year getting her settled and happy in her environment.

Yes, I do intend finding something to do. And this is the most exciting news. Cedric has agreed that as soon as we have found a place to live, I can finish my studies at the Ananda Ashram in India, where they have facilities to take care of Seja. It is situated near the beach in a place called Chinnamudaliarchavady. I kid you not! I know how to spell and pronounce it because I spent several weeks there a few years ago. I should be able to complete my studies within a year, and then I will be able to start my own yoga school and travel to various places giving classes and workshops. It's what I have always wanted to do and it's probably the only thing I can do without a work permit.

What do you mean, what will happen to my marriage? It will survive. Yogis don't have to be celibate, you know. I'm hoping Cedric will see the light and follow my path.

But now I do not want to discuss this any further. It's a life-changing situation and I'm becoming too emotional even talking about it.

The vibe in the room suddenly changed as each of us became pre-occupied with her own thoughts. I closed my eyes and visualised the scene in which the man, woman and child arrive in the crime-infested city of Chicago in midwinter, without friends, family, a home or sufficient money to keep them warm. The prospect of a job in some incomprehensible world of design technology is too vague for me to contemplate. With the man's connections in Italy, his passion for pasta and Sicilian sauces, the likelihood is that this new company is Mafia-owned, and it scares me. The forlorn family of new immigrants, having become accustomed to the grime and gloom of the historical but familiar architecture of London, is compelled to readjust to the stark and ugly low-cost tenement buildings in the slums – their only affordable accommodation. I picture them tramping through the sludge and sleet on slippery pavements in their English-made leather shoes and their London woollen overcoats, snatching greasy meals at deli-diners and buying cheap second-hand furnishings for their dimly-lit one-room apartment on the fourteenth floor overlooking uncollected garbage bins. They are cold, unhappy and desperate. It seems unlikely that they will be able to get out of their miserable surroundings to find their place in the sun, or the promised peace and fulfilment of the ashram on the shore of rural India, located far from the abject poverty and teeming masses of the cities.

I must have sighed deeply several times, because Rebecca was obviously waiting for me to gather myself together before she gave us her newsflash:

> What marvellous news. I have always wanted to go to Chicago to visit its great art museums. And, as it happens, Northwestern University has the best papermaking laboratories in the States. I will now be able to go via Chicago, instead of New York, on my way to Ecuador, where I will be working for a year.

Sarah and Rebecca, you both leapt out of your chairs and rushed to hug each other, shrieking with delight and dancing a kind of weird jig while throwing your arms in all directions. Hardly a graceful demonstration for adult women! I thought it quite tasteless in the context of this momentous announcement. Only when you both quietened down could we find out what Rebecca was talking about as she began answering the questions we threw at her:

> I know our Geography is poor. Blame it on the school system. But you are right – Ecuador is in South America. Yes, it's on the equator. I am going to be right near the Amazon forest in a district called Cotacachi. My wildest dream come true: I will be living in a small isolated vil-

lage in the valley of the Andes mountains – a place with an unpronounceable name, but in English it means 'Garden of Gethsemane.' They have started an amazing project to make paper from cabuya plant fibre, a substance similar to sisal fibre, which, as you know, after it's cooked and beaten, can be made into rope and coffee sacks.

Oh, you didn't know? Well, I'm sorry. I suppose it was presumptuous of me. If you are not papermakers, how would you know?

And what will I be doing there? I have been given a research grant to study the industry and make recommendations to the government to set up papermaking projects in several rural areas, particularly in KwaZulu/Natal, Mpumlanga and the Eastern Cape. I will be working with the local people in the Cotacachi area, and our aim will be to revitalise the demand for cabuya fibre by making pulp and handmade paper. This will help create jobs and generate an income for sixteen hundred families. I have been told that an international development organisation has come up with the idea of making fertilizer from the waste product. Isn't this a brilliant idea? The fertilizer-making process will be labour-intensive and will teach people additional skills that will bring in further income. All this will fit in perfectly with poverty-alleviation projects for our own rural areas in South Africa. So I intend learning everything I can to bring these ideas back home.

Where will I live? There is a basic kind of hut owned by a

woman, who apparently puts up foreigners when they come to this area.

No, Mom, I don't believe they have running water. There is a problem with water in the area, as the nearby rivers, where they wash the toxic cabuya fibres, are contaminated. They say all the fish have been killed off. It's one of the hazards that the people working with the fibre are covered in allergic rashes. But it rains every day, so I suppose I can wash in the rain and use some protective cream. Everyone walks around in gumboots because of the wet and muddy conditions, so at least you won't have to worry about my feet getting wet.

I'm afraid there are no modern conveniences, and I agree that long-drop toilets are not exactly my idea of fun. But I suppose I will get used to them. The good news is that there are solar panels in the hut, so one can cook food – but no, I don't know what kind of food I will be eating.

There are rough wooden bunks in the hut – and if it's not too hot and humid, I can always crawl into my sleeping bag.

Yes, Mom, there are snakes and creepy-crawlies. They tell me the leguaans in the swamps are so huge that they walk on two legs. It should be really interesting to see them, but I don't intend getting too close to them!

You asked about the people, Rachel. They are mostly Mestizo Indians, a mix of Indian and Spanish blood. Their ancestors, I believe, were from the Mayan and

Aztec cultures. They were colonised by the Spanish, so most people speak Spanish. I suppose I will have to learn some rudiments of the language to communicate on a basic level, but you know how hopeless I am at languages.

Mom, why are you crying? It's going to be the experience of a lifetime and will probably change the direction of my life. At the moment, I am incredibly frustrated teaching in an institution that refuses to transform itself. I am tired of begging for money from the Department of Arts and Culture for community art projects that should be on the department's list of priorities. I am sick of fighting the system – it's a losing battle. This is a hands-on opportunity for me to make a difference to some really poor communities, and I can bring home to South Africa the skills I learn, as well as some invaluable experience.

I tried to control myself, but each time I thought of my daughter in the swamps near the Amazon jungle, covered in red weals all over her body, ill with recurring malaria and amoebic dysentery, working in hazardous conditions with the hostile cabuya plant, unable to communicate with her fellow workers who were used to these hardships, I burst into tears. How will she survive in these conditions? How will she prevent dehydration when drinking water is scarce? Ecuador is a place that no one ever visits. Most people don't even know where it is or how near it is to Colombia, one of the major centres of the international drug trade. They may force her to peddle drugs for a few luxuries like soap, sugar and salt. They may even smuggle cocaine in her luggage when she returns to Johannesburg, a favourite airport for the drug trade.

And, if she gets ill in Cotacachi, how am I supposed to get there to look after her? What about visits from Trish, who hates being in places that do not have good accommodation and the comforts of modern living? She can't tolerate heat and is terrified of all crawling creatures. What about Rebecca's job, the first she has ever had that provides her with a steady income, security and respectability?

But I was not able to dwell any longer on the nightmarish South American scenario. You, Rachel, my youngest and usually the most pragmatic of my daughters, were anxious to have your say. Had I not been sitting down, I would certainly have fallen down when you, in your quiet but forceful way, began speaking:

> This is remarkable timing. There must be something after all in what they say about the psyche of families composed of women. Often their menstrual cycles coincide, either because of their genetics or because they are in harmony with each other. I came here with my newborn baby, my husband and my son, not only for the Batmitzvah celebration and our reunion, but because I felt the need to discuss with you all where my life is going and what I want to do with it.

> From the time I left school, I have had to work hard on myself, especially after the accident, and, for the past seven years, on others. I chose to work with abused women and children because I feel their need is greatest. I have been spending time and energy in impoverished communities, trying to educate teachers, social workers and parents.

> I now think I am suffering from burn-out. I don't want

to do that work anymore. I want to do only what is good for me and what will make me grow – and, of course, what is good for my husband and children. I want to sell everything – the house, the car, my practice, all our possessions – and move to a remote part of the country and live quietly and contentedly for the rest of my days. We can live off what we grow, and I can make crafts which we can sell. I no longer want the hassles of city life and the daily struggle of my profession.

Rebecca and Sarah, you jumped up to embrace Rachel. You all had broad grins on your faces. Looking smug, you three started whispering among yourselves – just out of my hearing range, which always annoys me intensely. Leah, meanwhile, was sitting quietly with a worried and perplexed look on her face. I looked to her for support, but she averted her gaze.

I began to rationalise: Rachel is tired and probably suffering from post-natal depression. We all seem to go through a stage in our lives in which we want to throw off our daily routine and go into the wilderness. I used to dream about going to Hawaii, picturing the empty sun-drenched beaches, waving palm trees, huge waves crashing on the shore. I would live in a wooden hut near the beach, swimming out in the calm turquoise waters of the ocean, surfing with the dolphins in the late afternoon, living off fish and local produce the islanders would sell to me. I would have books, music and a typewriter. I needed nothing else. Neither husband nor children came into my equation. My beautiful dream was shattered some years ago when I visited Hawaii – a tourist trap of American high-rise hotels and shopping centres.

Perhaps Rachel's vision of an idyllic life in a peaceful part of our country is similar to my Hawaiian dream – illusionary, impractical and ridiculous. She has two children and a husband to consider. She has responsibilities and can't go rushing off to nothing. The only flaw in my reasoning is Rachel herself. She is not prone to fantasy or idle chatter. She confirmed this as she continued with her speech:

> Yes, Leah, I'm not forgetting that Eli, on the other hand, is very keen on immigrating to Australia. He has discussed this many times with you and Sam. We would love our children to grow up together, to really know one another and have the support of an extended family which is so vital to all of us. He has discussed the possibility of joining Sam in his computer venture, and they think that by combining their individual skills, they could create a successful partnership. He was the one to persuade me to come here so that we can seriously consider our options.

But before Rachel was able to continue her explanation, Leah jumped up, pale and trembling, and in an agitated tone said:

> No, no, you can't do that. You can't come to Australia. I didn't want to spoil our reunion by telling you of our plans, but it seems I have no choice now. The children, Sam and I have finally decided that we are making *aliyah* to Israel. We have been discussing this for a long time and, although we have been successful and happy in Perth, our dream has always been to immigrate to Israel. This is where our spiritual home is.

She looked around at each of us before continuing:

As you can imagine, this has been an enormously difficult decision for us. But we have now made up our
minds. No, you can't persuade us to reconsider, even
though we – and the children – have developed close and
meaningful friendships which have sustained us during
our time here. In the absence of family we have forged a
strong support base among some incredible people. In
fact, when we mentioned the possibility of leaving Perth,
there was a pall over the community, and we have not
had the courage to broach the subject again. I now will
have to accept that I have reached a stage in my life
where I need to be on the receiving side.

A broad smile appeared on Rachel's face. She put her hands
together in the yogic prayer position and emitted a ululation of
approval. Leah responded rather sharply:

Why are you carrying on like that, Rachel? Are you
happy about our decision? Did you not want to come to
Perth? Did you really dupe Eli into believing that you
were agreeable to immigrating to Australia even though
you had concocted other plans? Is it possible that he fell
into the trap you set – that if something untoward happened to prevent your immigration here, he would agree
to an alternative place to live? Yes, I know how much you
love South Africa and that you have often said how you
would hate to leave. But you have certain obligations to
your children to let them grow up where it is safe for
them. Yes, I know I sound upset because in all the years
we begged you to come, you always refused. Now that we
are leaving, you tell us that you are considering a move
here. What took you so long? But apart from all that,

please, Rachel, tell us you are not serious about wanting to live in the midlands of Kwa-Zulu/Natal – the middle of nowhere.

Knowing her eldest sister's weaknesses, Rachel decided to use a similar form of attack:

And why not, Leah? It seems that you think it perfectly viable for your family to go to Israel – to give up your comfort, security and everything you have worked so hard for in the Perth community to go to nothing. How are you going to manage without a support base? Where are you going to live? How will you and Sam support your children? How will you manage with the language? Do you think you will adjust to the culture and customs of the Israelis?

Leah, feeling the hostility, took a deep breath, bracing herself to defend her position:

Well, we have several choices. We can go on *aliyah* to an *ulpan* – an absorption centre where the Israeli govern-ment assists new immigrants with airfares, accommoda-tion, learning Hebrew and finding jobs. It will be a tough way to do it because if we can't make a go of it, we have to repay back the loan and we will have lost time and money – in the long term it becomes a costly exercise. Our second choice, which we think will be a better option and a softer landing for our family, is to go to a religious *yishuv*, a settlement called Alon Shfut – 'the Foot of the Tree' – in the *gush*. The settlement lies in Israeli-occupied territory, about fifty miles north of Jerusalem.

Yes, it is quite safe there, especially since they've built a new road to the area, as well as a tunnel under the mountain, which is guarded day and night by Israeli soldiers.

No, it doesn't belong to the Palestinians. The land was occupied by Israel before the '67 war, although it doesn't belong to Israel. It's a kind of no man's land, so property is free.

We will be able to rent a very nice but affordable house. The children can go either to local schools or to yeshivas in Jerusalem. The synagogue is a five-minute walk from the house, the bus stop is close and most of the people speak English. It's a young community with people of similar religious convictions and strong commitments to the land and to their families. So, it should not be a complete culture shock for us or the children.

My head was pounding as new thoughts erupted in my mind. It was hard enough for me to deal with Leah's Orthodox observances while living in Perth, but to be living on the outskirts of Jerusalem in a religious community on occupied land is a different matter. Imagine being greeted by a friendly wave of an Uzi machine-gun as the Israeli soldiers beckon the family through the barricade to their new home in the Judean hills, far from the hum of city life. I shudder to think of the buses being searched for weapons as the children go to school or on an educational excursion to some historical sight – an easy target for unhappy dissidents wishing to wreak mayhem on innocent people. My beloved ones, unable to speak the language and express their feelings adequately, can only pretend to be having a good time and adjusting to the strange behaviour of their foreign brethren.

I can visualise my hard-working daughter confined to the house, mooching around in a long cumbersome colourless dress, her beautiful long *shaytel* stuffed into a hideous hat, which all the women seem to wear to cover their hair, with a pink rose in the front to soften the unflattering shape. With no make-up and looking pale and wan, she can barely hide her tears as the children cling to her skirts, sobbing and begging to go back to the life they loved in Australia, where people cared for and understood them. All day long she is baking bread, cooking and cleaning while listening to Hebrew language tapes – intent on doing *mitzvot* for people she hardly knows. Meanwhile, Sam, having grown a full beard, is walking the streets of Jerusalem dressed in his white shirt, black trousers and black wide-brimmed hat, his *tzitzit* hanging out of his trousers, trying to find work or raise money to support his family. Without knowing how to communicate or behave appropriately, he is defeated before he begins.

And it's probably all my fault. Did I not tell Sam that Leah needed psychological help because of her abundant hospitality – her chronic need to feed and take care of people? It is now obvious to me that she wishes to run away from her addiction, little realising that unless she deals with it appropriately, it will follow her wherever she goes. And, in Israel, she certainly won't have the means to indulge her habit.

Sarah was the first to express our doubts and fears:

> You can't go to Israel. There are too many problems
> there. I would feel very uncomfortable about your move.
> I have such mixed feelings about the politics and the

people. I don't believe there will ever be peace there. It is
not safe for your children – and don't forget they are my
nieces and nephews. It will be alienating for all of us. You
will be sucked into a religious community with their
strict observances restricting what you can and cannot
do. You will reject your secular family, especially your
sisters who are on different paths. You will become
embroiled in political debates and controversial party
politics – and you know how I feel about the land issues.
We will not be able to identify with you and support
you. You may even start judging us. Apart from that, it is
selfish to uproot the children. The next thing we'll hear
is that they will join the army after they finish school.
And you know how we all feel about guns and war!

We all started talking at the same time, all shocked that Leah, the
eldest of the family, the level-headed one, the ideal role model, the
mediator and peacemaker, should be embarking on such a radical
course. Where was her sense of responsibility? It was a question in
all our minds, but it was onto me that she turned her anger:

Mom, you of all people should support us. How many
times did you say that it doesn't make sense to immigrate anywhere else in the world? Weren't you sincere
about that? Did you say it only because you thought we
would never actually go to Israel? Don't you know that it
is the best place to bring up children? Have you forgotten that the society revolves around the children because
the future of the Jews and the Jewish state depends on
them? Don't you remember that my dream is to have the
family in one place so that my children can be close to
my sisters? If we make our home there, maybe my sisters

will join us one day. But in the meantime, Israel is only eight hours away from Johannesburg and en route to everywhere. We will be able to have Pesach and Rosh Hashanah together. Just think how much easier our future reunions will be.

Considering the practical implications of this move for our scattered family, I felt duly chastised, though highly anxious about the volatile situation in the Middle East. Peace in Israel seems to be a pipe dream, and the idea of my children and grandchildren in a war zone was unbearable. But we had momentarily forgotten that Rachel had not yet filled us in on the details of her plans. It was Leah who reminded us, querying with a measure of sarcasm:

Tell us, Rachel, what has got into you to make you want to uproot your husband and children to go into the remote regions of South Africa so that you can 'find yourself'.

Rachel got that look on her face we all hate, as if to say, 'Don't argue with me.' She is headstrong and obstinate, and gives the impression that she knows better than anyone else what is good for her. People have told me such behaviour is typical of a fourth-child syndrome. She could always see through things. I could never tell her anything unless she was convinced that I knew what I was talking about. Phrases such as 'Do this' or 'Don't do that' were anathema to her. She did not like discipline. Even when she was lying in hospital for five weeks after her accident and had to undergo surgery and countless skin grafts while in traction for her injured spine, she refused to compromise or to be controlled by the doctors until she was convinced that they knew what they were doing. She refused palliatives and painkillers, mustering a self-control and courage not dissimilar to that which she deployed during the home birth. So now, we were all dreading what she was going to say:

> Ever since I can remember, I have been interested in techniques of healing. I have loved being a therapist and believe I have treated my clients with some success. But it's not enough for me. For years I have been reading about healing and studying it, and in the process have met some incredible African healers. I am sure you have all heard of Credo Mutwa, the most well-known sangoma, healer and spiritual leader in South Africa. I have brought his book with me so that I can share his insights with you. But we'll do that later. For now, let me quote something from the first chapter which is indelibly printed on my mind. He says, 'My becoming a sangoma … was a journey of searching for the great truth, a journey of being healed by greater healers than I, of my many ailments, and also, eventually healing others of my people when I myself became a fully-fledged healer.' That's what I want to do.

Everyone was speechless. As for me, this announcement exceeded my wildest imaginings. My child wanting to follow in the footsteps of a Zulu shaman, throwing bones and making vile concoctions with animal intestines, roots and plants to ward off evil spirits. It's an impossible notion. What kind of bizarre hallucination was I living through? I visualised Rachel sitting bare-breasted in front of her mud kraal, with her hair in dreadlocks and beads and her face painted in warrior colours, beating drums while chanting weird incantations. Her husband, wearing only a black Speedo and a beaded sweatband, is stirring the mealie porridge with a

144

long wooden spoon to feed their barefoot children clad in loin-cloths made from animal skins and rags. Several groups of people have gathered near her hut, patiently waiting to be treated by the white sangoma, believing that her brand of medicine will cure their hunger and hardship. Apart from the heat and flies, this scene, in one of the beautiful valleys of a thousand hills, has a feeling of peace and tranquillity. But it's certainly not a place I want to be!

My reverie was disturbed by Leah, who leapt out of her chair as though she had been sitting on red-hot coals:

> What happened to your Jewish upbringing, your religious convictions, your value system and your resolve to give your son a Jewish education? Are you going to throw away your life's work for some crazy idea? Has a witch doctor put a *tokoloshe* in your house to bewitch you?

Rachel, who appeared to be enjoying the furore she was causing, replied calmly:

> Why are you so hysterical, Leah? To become a sangoma I don't have to give up my Judaism. It has nothing to do with religion. In the same way Sarah can become a yogi without compromising her Jewish roots and upbringing. It brings another dimension to Judaism and, if anything, will strengthen my belief system. For example, the Zulu version of meditation teaches you to breathe softly and gently like a whisper until you feel something like a hot coiled snake ascending your spine and bursting through the top of your head. It's called *umbilini*, not unlike *kun-*

dalini in yoga, which we have all practiced together. In the Kabbalah it is called *devekut* – the union of 'kisses' that unites 'breath to Breath', where one achieves a state of deep and passionate cleaving to G-d. So whatever form it takes, whether it is Eastern, Western, African, Jewish or personal, meditation frees the mind to experience infinite depth and spiritual awareness. You, Leah, are going to be following a spiritual path in Israel, and I will be following a spiritual path in Africa. It's only the methods that differ. I will become a Jewish sangoma!

Rebecca was staring at her sister in disbelief as she said:

There is no way you can become a sangoma, Jewish or otherwise. You should know that a sangoma's power is based on traditional healing whereby knowledge is passed on secretly from father to son, or in some cases from mothers to daughters. Fundamental to the power of the sangoma is the ability to call upon the ancestors to intervene. Ancestor worship is therefore an essential part of the process. Do you intend to call up your Jewish ancestors to help you diagnose ailments, chase away evil spirits, exorcise demons and then mix potions and remedies to cure people? Have you forgotten that you are descended from Shneur Zalman of Liadi, the famous rabbi who founded the Chasidic movement?

Rebecca and Rachel seldom argue, but this was incitement.

Rebecca, what gives you the right to say those things to me? What makes you think it's OK for you to go off into the Amazon jungle and live with the American Indians,

while it's strange behaviour for me to stay in my country
and find out about the Zulu people and their culture?
Even if I can't become a full-fledged sangoma because of
my unsuitable ancestors, I'm sure I will learn enough to
find alternative ways of healing.

And you, Sarah, do you think because you are six years
older than me and have always taken it upon yourself to
look after me, that it's fine for you to go to India to learn
how to heal yourself and others through yoga because
it's more universal and acceptable? You, of all people,
who devoted yourself to the struggle in our country,
have suddenly forgotten the real wisdom of Africa and
its magical and mystical mythology.

And you, Mom, who taught us to be freethinkers and
gave us wings, look as though you are in the middle of a
catastrophe. You should be rejoicing. Your four daughters have found what they really want in life and are
going to live accordingly. Suddenly you no longer like all
the wild stuff you've taught us. You no longer want us to
run with the wolves. You thought we wouldn't have the
guts to follow through, so you kept telling us folk tales.
In fact, you relied on the assumption that we would
never do what you said we should do. As long as it is the-
oretical and in the realms of philosophy, you approve. As
soon as it becomes a reality, you don't like it anymore.
You could not have been sincere in your desires for us.
You thought that you would always be able to guide us,
to teach us and above all to control us. Well, you no
longer can. We are wild women and you cannot tame us.
We are off to follow our dreams.

Was it a sob I tried to suppress, or was it the sound of the blood rushing through my veins? I felt my heart palpitating and my stomach churning as I heard Rebecca say:

> Mom, are you worried about what will happen to you without your daughters around you? You are lucky you have had us under your wings for so long. Now you will have to learn to fly without us. Why are you suddenly feeling so helpless and alone?

It dawned on me that I was never able to teach my daughters to give me the respect I am entitled to as their mother. I had always hoped it would come naturally, without coercion. I was obviously wrong. After everything I had done for them, I did not deserve to be cast aside so callously, to be left to my own devices while they prepared to take off in four different directions. Not one of them considered my feelings, let alone made plans to accommodate me in their new lifestyles. Did I not devote myself selflessly and tirelessly to them and their families? Was I not a caring and available mother and grandmother? How could my altruistic actions have backfired so dismally?

This, my dear daughters, was my state of mind when heavy-heartedly I boarded the flight from Perth to Johannesburg. As you can imagine I was shaken, disappointed and wracked with self-pity. My expectations of our reunion were disappointed. My role as a Jewish mother had not only drastically changed, but had almost become redundant. My children no longer needed my advice, my experience, my teachings or my guidance.

That was the thought that obsessed me on the flight home. The on-flight movies I had looked forward to had lost their appeal. The food seemed more unappetizing than usual, and the person assigned to sit next to me on those ill-designed reclining seats was an evil-smelling Australian goat farmer who kept telling me that certain breeds of South African goats are the best in the world. I could neither confirm nor deny it as I know nothing about goats. Most of the information he gave me was unintelligible because of his broad outback accent, and so I lost an opportunity to learn more about goat breeding on a global scale, which would have taken my mind off family problems. On arrival, an interminable delay in getting our baggage from the aircraft convinced me that I no longer wished to travel abroad.

I did not willingly succumb to my breakdown. Circumstances forced me into it. I could not avoid my anxiety attacks and the recurring nightmares of the demons inhabiting my daughters' lives. Any self-respecting conscientious Jewish mother would have suffered a similar collapse.

So, my darling daughters, while my love for all of you is unconditional and constant, I think it fair to tell you that I am bitterly disappointed in the decisions you have made for your life changes.

Much love
Mom

9 October

My darling Leah, Rebecca, Rachel and Sarah

Until now I have not felt like answering your postcards and e-mails from your various destinations. I am certainly glad that you have each managed 'to do your thing' without coming to any harm. I am feeling much stronger and more focused now since my recovery. I must thank you all for the good vibes you have sent me and for the individual meditations you devoted so conscientiously to my recovery.

My problem is now solved: no more reunions! I have had in-depth discussions with my psychoanalyst, my psychotherapist, my kinesiologist, my cardiologist and my swimming instructor (who specialises in teaching dolphin breathing) and, after much deliberation, they have ruled that my mental and physical state will not be able to withstand another reunion. In fact, they have suggested banning the word reunion from my vocabulary and recommended a cybertherapist to alarm my keyboard if I should, inadvertently, be tempted to use it.

I am sure that you well understand the reasons for my serious destabilisation. After all, it was our previous get-together in Betty's Bay which probably precipitated me into my momentous decision to end my thirty-seven-year marriage. While none of the team of consultants could actually pinpoint the blame on our family gathering, they do not rule out its insidious influence. Their opinion was that the Betty's Bay meeting may well have brought about 'the-straw-that-broke-the-camel's-back-syndrome' – an unfortunate and unflattering description – whereas the Marapana Wildlife Lodge get-together was responsible for my physical and nervous collapse. They perceived that it was triggered by severe shock – four shocks, in fact. Although the acute phase of this illness has almost passed, they urged me to avoid a repetition of this situation, and I'm assured that, provided I remain in long-term intensive therapy, there is every chance that I will continue to live a normal and fairly cheerful life.

I have been given a written report by one of the consultants, Dr Dvorki, who became interested in the unusual nature of my case. He is not only an expert in social syndromes but is also an amateur Jewish historian. If, in spite of its length and obscure and incomprehensible language, any of you would like to see the document, I will e-mail it to you as an attachment. (I know how to do that now.) He describes the acute phase of this Jewish mother–daughter syndrome in some detail and notes that it is usually activated by disturbing behaviour on the part of one, or at most two, daughters. In my case, where four daughters simultaneously activated the syndrome, the outcome was better than he could have anticipated. He gave me an alarming account of one of his cases, in which the mother's life was under threat and she had to flee from her daughter's wrath. There is apparently a long history of Jewish mother–daughter syndrome dating back to biblical times and therefore he was particularly interested in the names I had chosen for my daughters. The statistics show that Jewish mothers have apparently always had innately cherished and excessive expectations of their daughters, and when these expectations are not met, the incipient syndrome first presents itself in a mild and harmless form – often described in layman's terms as 'nagging'. This manifestation tends to increase in intensity and frequency, resulting in hypertension, raised voices and irrational behaviour where the subject starts interfering with the activities of her offspring. Very often an authoritarian and dictatorial attitude is displayed, culminating in hostile attitudes and adult temper tantrums.

Interestingly, he noted that the behavioural deviations of my daughters had tended to strengthen rather than weaken our relationships. After my five sessions on his couch he confidently pronounced – to my relief – that, until the damaging episode of 'the get-together', there was a healthy balance and harmony in our interactions with each other. Dr Dvorki postulated that if I had been better prepared for the unexpected turn of events through appropriate counselling before my traumatic encounter with my daughters, my coping mechanisms might have sustained me. Due to the advances in the treatment of this syndrome – known by specialists in the field as P.M.J.M.D.S. (postmodern Jewish mother–daughter syndrome) – preventive measures can and must be put into place before a confrontation occurs.

Apparently, it was the surprise element that caused the damage. I had led my life in a certain way because of my expectations. Having brought up my daughters within a clearly defined value system, I expected a particular type of behaviour. I was under the impression we were firmly rooted in the real world. By giving you all a sense of self, free to choose to be what you wanted to be, I admit that I lapsed into a state of complacency after you turned thirty, an age of sense and sensibility. Terms such as maturity, social responsibility, personal commitment, financial accountability and family loyalty spring to mind. Please note that I have not mentioned your filial obligations, your debts of gratitude, your duty-bound obedience nor the biblical injunction to 'honour thy mother'. At Marapana Wildlife Lodge, it was as though each one of you, on your maniacal missions to forge a new future for yourselves, disregarded your past and your present and everything I had ever taught you. In your haste to reach your self-absorbed goals, you shattered my peace of mind, destroyed my ambition for your success and radically removed whatever chance I had of *kleibing nachas* from my children, and their children, in my twilight years.

Yes, my darling daughters, separately and collectively, you have suddenly become creatures over whom I have no control. Shedding the familiar, the constant, your comforts, goals, friends, families and countries, you have decided to break loose. I admit that I recommended that you read *Women who Run with the Wolves* by Clarissa Pinkola Estes, but at no stage did I imagine that you would actually follow the philosophy of instinct and, what is more, all decide to do it at the same time. It seems that just as I had you all figured out, you decide to run off, clear out, turn a new page, break the rules and stop the world. I do not agree with Estes, who is not only a Jungian analyst but a teller of archetypal folk tales, when she says: 'The wild teacher, wild mother, wild mentor supports their inner and outer lives, no matter what.' Let me assure you that I do not support your wild ways in spite of her explanation that *wild* in its original sense means 'to live a natural life … with healthy boundaries'. How is a mother supposed to bear this? How can she stand by and witness her offspring, whom she has nurtured with loving care and kindness, running off into the unknown to follow bizarre dreams and madness, leaving their mother behind? Perhaps Clarissa Pinkola Estes with her Mexican-

Spanish bloodline is more stoical than I could ever be, an ordinary Jewish mother with Lithuanian–South African forebears.

Anyway, you surely see, my dear children, how potentially damaging further 'family-togetherness' ventures would be for me. I will visit you all from time to time on a one-on-one basis. I could be persuaded to arrange for two of you to be in the same place at the same time to cut down on expenses, but no more. It is painful for me to admit to you my lack of emotional and physical stamina, but it seems I have been beaten at my own game.

Much love
Mom

12 November

My darling daughters

Look for the paperclip – this is my first attachment!

Never before has a Jewish mother enjoyed such a variety of healers to cure her ailments. I am sure it helped, particularly as there was such a wide range and choice of forms of spiritual healing from different sources – the shores of India, the jungles of Ecuador, the Western Wall of Jerusalem and the Transkei/KwaZulu midlands of South Africa.

However, I did not rely entirely on your spiritual meditations or your emotionally charged warm wishes for my recovery. While I was undergoing various medical treatments and therapies, I took the precaution of getting help from a cyberguru as well. Do you remember me telling you about my American tenant, born in India, who lives in the garden cottage? Well, apart from being a really nice young man – a bit untidy, I admit – Siddhartha is a computer boffin. After witnessing my distress following my sojourn down under, he persuaded me to confide in him and tell him what had led to my sad state of mind – visible in my drawn face, the black rings under my eyes and my weight loss. Obviously, I could not tell him everything, but I told him enough to elicit his sympathy.

He generously offered me cybertherapy, a brand-new type of alternative healing recommended for ambitious young people who are unable to keep up with the bombardment of new software programmes in the workplace. While he admitted that I did not fit into this category, he agreed to modify the treatment for my specific needs. He suggested an amicable financial arrangement whereby I reduce the rental of the cottage to pay for his services. While this is not ideal for practical reasons, such as paying the bills, I believe the long-term advantages are worth the economic strain. Until my discussions with Siddhartha, I had thought my problems insoluble.

I have great confidence in Siddhartha because on a previous occasion he saved me from an extremely stressful situation. Shortly after I acquired my laptop, the built-in mouse started throwing my words into gobbledegook each time I struck a key. The service technicians and computer companies I called were unable to cure this strange malady. I was prepared to give up my lovely laptop because of the anxiety it was causing me. With uncanny timing, Siddhartha appeared like Sir Lancelot on his white steed to perform a most noble deed and rescue my computer from an untimely end. Having immediately grasped the problem, he jumped into his fiery-red Jetta, and raced to his office to retrieve a spare external mouse and mousepad for my little laptop. No sooner had he connected the new mouse than my words appeared on the screen in standard English.

The current problem requires a more subtle solution. He is using a holistic approach to treat my communication block which was triggered by the Jewish mother–daughter syndrome. It is a combination of Buddhist philosophy and new-age technology. Its success is overwhelming – no sooner had I started the therapy then I started feeling calmer. My nervousness and fears no longer threaten my daily routine. His suggestion is that we deal with this block in a rational and technological way – through 'attachments', the simple basic function key on the e-mail programme. Before this, I was writing long e-mails to each of you, most of which took me several days, and it was a matter of luck whether I was able to save them. On many occasions they disappeared without a trace and, provided I had the time and energy, I would have to begin again. Sometimes they showed up in the in-box without a subject, or appeared mysteriously in the out-box even though I hadn't knowingly sent them there. The frustration was enormous and, let me add, it usually happened to the most important and longest letters. I often tried to copy and paste the saved letter, but the formatting was unruly because the e-mail programme is not the same as my word-processing programme. It was easier to delete a sloppy-looking message than to correct it. Needless to say, the technical difficulties in writing lengthy e-mails letters to you caused me heart palpitations and nervous tremors. Yet, as soon as I mastered the technique of 'attaching' my documents, I felt safe and secure, and suffused with a lightness of being. Now I am able to write as much as I like, press the paperclip icon on the tool bar, and my letter to my daughters is attached. Then I have the freedom to send it whenever I want.

I think it fair to pass on the warning Siddhartha gave me about avoiding mail-merge, which, while seemingly performing a similar function to attachments, is dangerous if it puts your address into the wrong hands. There are people out there waiting to advertise their wares, bombard you with useless information, coerce you into joining the race to be in the right place at the right time for the new millennium and becoming a millionaire. He is particularly wary of that pernicious and contagious scourge the chain letter, often disseminated through mail-merge. He strongly advises you never to read those letters that begin 'This is not a chain letter …'. The writer then proceeds to tell you a heartbreaking story about a boy dying of cancer in the most dire circumstances, who might be helped if there were any decent people left in this world, followed by good wishes for your own health, and a promise that if you circulate this letter among your friends and acquaintances, it will not only help the boy's chances to live but will bring you health and good fortune because you are such a caring person. If, on the other hand, you choose to ignore the letter, the writer sadly reminds that you have made the choice to invite doom into your life. The strange rationale of the chain letter is that, however much it irritates you, however logical you are, however firm your decision is not to impose this curse on others, including people you don't like, it invariably wakes you up in the middle of the night with an eerie sense of your own vulnerability and inadequacy. The menacing question "What if … ?" hangs over you until morning.

Siddhartha was delighted when he heard that you all practice meditation in different ways and feels that the success of our attachment undertaking is assured by following a few basic procedures. He suggests that we devote ten minutes each morning to chanting a mantra, since, through the repetition of this word or phrase, we will gradually free our mind from the material world and reach a level of *samadhi* – a Sanskrit word for realisation – in cyberspace. In this way, when we use e-mail for cybercommunication we will have cleared all obstacles in our way. Obviously we need to be completely open and honest with one another, and are required to keep in regular e-mail contact disclosing our plans, probable actions, aspirations and ideas. We then 'attach' matters of importance and forward them to each other. It will help monitor any aberrations and behavioural abnormalities 'the other' may be undergoing, and may act as a deterrent against major upheavals in our family. I am optimistic that through this simple procedure, the special relationships I used to enjoy with my four daughters will be restored.

I visualise this as a stepping stone to our next phase. By using 'attachments' to maximum potential, we will be freeing ourselves for the realisation of my loftier vision for our mother–daughter correspondence. It is my fervent wish that we rise above the banal and commercial usages and work towards elevating e-mail to a new art form – we will create a literary genre of intimate e-mail letters. Not only will we be able to develop our communication skills on a higher level, but we will forge even closer attachments to each other that will in time transcend all adversity.

If you are agreeable to this proposal, I may reconsider and undertake another reunion after all. Benjamin has invited me to his Barmitzvah celebration in Israel, in the new millennium. He is, after all, my eldest grandson and he wants me to be there with him. I would not dream of disappointing him and I have already told him that I would not miss it for the world. In the meantime, I appreciate the assurances you have expressed in your e-mails to me that our next get-together need not necessarily be so traumatic for me. Of course you are right.

Much love
Mom

17 December

My darling daughters

Voila! Another attachment. You will all be receiving the same news at the same time.

Much has happened since my last e-mail to you. But let me start at the beginning – usually a good place to begin a story. Of course I don't mean the beginning of my life or yours, I mean the beginning of my journey into cyberspace.

As you know the recovery from my nervous breakdown was due in large measure to the intensive and costly therapy programmes I underwent, in particular the successful one devised by Siddhartha. As I gradually freed myself from my inhibitions and fears, and gained more courage, self-confidence and familiarity with my laptop, I ventured out alone into the World Wide Web. Prior to this, as you well know, I had only used the Internet to communicate with you and a few friends via e-mail. Had I not undergone cybertherapy I may have gone through the rest of my life ignorant of the joys and riches offered by the Web and those search engines that can change your life.

One night, several months ago, I was feeling particularly lonely as I sat at my desk surfing the Net. I had not lowered the blinds, because I was watching a dramatic summer lightning storm streaking across the black sky. The thunder was menacing before the rain came pelting down, and although I had been warned to switch off my computer during a storm, I needed the comfort and company of the screen. It may have been a flash of lightning that triggered that intuitive spark within me, but suddenly I found myself involuntarily searching the Web for Sean Asher Chan Salamon. He is a marine biologist whose research and photography of whales in the Arctic Circle has intrigued me for years. I have all his books in my library and have spent hours pondering whether the flukes of the whales reflect the light of the sunset or whether he used certain darkroom techniques to capture their elusive magnificence against the backdrop of gigantic glaciers.

You have all heard me talking for years about watching whales in Antarctica. The idea remained in the realms of my dreams – only occasionally emerging into the real world when people made fun of my passion for Moby Dick, my white whale – always more real than mythical for me. I knew that a trip to Antarctica would be an indulgence I could neither afford nor justify, besides which my circulatory system is so poor that I get chilblains in the South African winter.

That stormy night I found a whale-watching site on the Web that provided me with some intriguing information. But the miraculous part of the story is that I located the e-mail address of my hero, Sean Asher Chan Salamon, described on the Net as the 'prize-winning photographer and world-famous researcher'. Before losing my nerve, and the Web site, I impulsively resolved to contact him and wrote him a long e-mail. I told him about my passion for whales, particularly humpbacks. And I told him about the two I regard as my family, having adopted them in Cape Cod, with the blessings of Greenpeace.

This was the beginning of a correspondence the likes of which I had never imagined. I was soon calling him Charlie – the name his Canadian friends affectionately call him by – and our e-letters gained momentum. Apart from his quick wit and hilarious sense of humour, he is a kind, highly intelligent and sensitive man. He is knowledgeable about many subjects and widely read in classical literature. I have learnt more about whale-watching from his letters than from all my numerous trips around Stellwagen Bay, the numerous sightings of the southern right from Betty's Bay, or the books I had read on the subject. His philosophical musings about whales and life touched me profoundly, because intuitively and instinctively I have felt this spiritual and emotional bonding with whales without being able to articulate it. His passion for whales also began with literature, and he is one of the few people I know who can recite whole passages from *Moby Dick*. Until then, I had almost given up on the male species.

After a while, we were exchanging little confidences about our lives. Besides books, we found many things in common, including music and art. And amazingly enough, Charlie too had been married for more than thirty years, although to three different wives. We are of a similar age, and he has four sons from two wives. They have sensible and well-paying professions: the eldest is a doctor, the second a lawyer, the third an accountant and the youngest a banker. Do you think they needed their respectability and anchoring in the real world because their father spent so much time floating under the water with oxygen tanks and underwater photographic equipment? (I must remember to ask him.) Perhaps that is why he became so intrigued by my relationship with my daughters. At first, I was reticent and reluctant to divulge too much about you, but he seemed to take a real delight in hearing about your various careers and how you all decided to quit what you were so successfully doing. He wholeheartedly approves of your wild adventures and admires the changes you have made in your lifestyles. He even congratulated me on my open-mindedness and free spirit that encouraged you to follow your dreams. I did not think it appropriate to tell him of my vehement disapproval of your actions and how it caused my nervous collapse.

He has an interesting lineage, as you can tell from his name. His grandfather on his mother's side was Jewish and lived in Shanghai until he fell in love with and married an Irish Catholic woman who converted to Judaism after their children were born. His grandmother on his father's side was a beautiful Chinese woman from an illustrious family who disgraced the family by marrying a Dutch engineer working in Malaysia. So you see, he is a mixture of four different cultures and languages. Which makes it even more amazing that he has taken an interest in me, an ordinary Jewish South African mother.

After several weeks of intense e-mail correspondence, Charlie issued me a challenge I couldn't refuse. He invited me to join his research team on an ice-breaker for three months to document the feeding habits of the humpback whales in a remote region of Alaska. I know it is not Antarctica, but he tells me that the region is uncharted, and the icebergs and glaciers are more breathtaking than those in Antarctica. I will only need to pay for my airfare to Vancouver because the passage on the ship is being sponsored by the *New Millennium Discovery* magazine. What is more, I will be provided with a full wardrobe of warm clothing including fur-lined boots, thermal underwear and a special jacket like those worn by Alaskans. Charlie thinks it unlikely that I will get frostbite. He has jocularly told me I need bring only a toothbrush, cosmetics, undergarments and vitamins.

If I agree, and I'm sure I will, we sail in four weeks' time. In all likelihood, unless there are unforeseen blizzards and ice floes that prevent our return passage, I will be back in good time to attend Benjamin's Barmitzvah in Israel.

It is unfortunate that, while in Alaska, I will not be able to communicate with you by e-mail, but with the state-of-the-art technology on the ship, we may be able to send and receive brief radio messages to each other.

I am so excited I can hardly type on. Like the wild woman who runs with the wolves, I will now realize the wildest fantasy of my life. Thank you for giving me the courage.

Much love
Mom

21 December

Leah, Rebecca, Rachel and Sarah

I cannot believe your reactions to my e-mail! You have never answered my letters so quickly before. Nor do I have any idea how you were able to make instant contact with one another and present me with this implacable united front.

What do you mean I can't go? Who are you to tell me what I can and cannot do? Why are you so shocked when I make decisions for myself that don't include you? And what do you mean by telling me that Jewish mothers don't behave like this and cannot go running off to the North Pole with a man they have never met? You talk about propriety – that it's not decent for a single woman to be on a ship for three months with a predominantly male crew. Well, why not? Am I suddenly not to be trusted? Am I not of an age that I have acquired enough experience to take care of myself?

Why do you ask me, 'What will people will say?' Did you care what they said when you all chose your unconventional lives? All I ever wanted was four nice Jewish kugels about whom I could boast to my friends. But you made me go into the closet with all your activities – religious, political, artistic and alternative.

Leah, you seem to be worried about how I will keep Shabbat on an ice-breaker in the middle of nowhere where, some of the time, the sun doesn't even set. Well, it's certainly a valid question. I will have to consult some of the rabbis to find out when I would light candles on Shabbat, and do various *brochas* and *mitzvot*, as I doubt whether there will be other Jews around. But I'm sure we'll sort something out. It is only temporary, and if it requires some extra effort, I will certainly do what I can. Charlie has been very open-minded about the food I intend eating and he has promised to order whatever I need. He has also suggested that I bring some special ingredients with me as he loves traditional Jewish cooking. Making a big *cholent* or chicken soup with *kneidlach*, or even *tzimmes* with carrots occasionally, for the captain, a few members of the crew and research team might be great fun. It will certainly keep us warm and content.

Rebecca, you seem to be concerned about my health and my bad circulation. As you know, I am very fit now and over all my coronary problems. I will take special precautions to boost my circulation and I believe there are excellent multivitamins that will provide everything my body needs. I will probably be in better health on the expedition than at home. There is also a ship's doctor who is qualified to deal with any contingency that may arise. He is Russian, and I have great faith in Russian doctors.

Sarah, I am flabbergasted at your prudish and moralistic concerns, and your value judgements. When you were underground for all those years, living on the edge with those unsavoury characters who were always being arrested and thrown into jail, I had to deal with it on my own, without letting on to anyone that you were involved with the ANC. And, when you married out of the faith, did I not give you my unstinting support? Now you are worried that because Charlie has such a mixed cultural background I will not be able to cope with it. You ask what I know about Asian culture, Dutch conservatism or fiery Irish temperament. Nothing, I suppose. But no doubt I will learn quickly. No, I have never been to Shanghai, Malaysia or Canada, nor to most of the other places he's lived in. Of course, I have never been deep-sea diving in the Pacific, the Atlantic or in fact any other ocean. You are absolutely right – I have never really experienced cold or discomfort, nor have I been anywhere without a family support system. It won't be easy and I will need to summon up my dormant resources.

Of all my daughters, I thought you, Rachel, who deals with people's minds and psyches on a daily basis, would understand my need to go on this whale-research expedition. Yet you give a hundred reasons for me not to go. You maintain that I first need to undergo more therapy, to prepare me for dealing with new and extreme changes. You even predict that the icy wasteland of Alaska will be traumatic for the mind and emotional health of someone like me, who loves the red African soil, the luscious vegetation, the colours of the landscape, the bright flowering trees and flowers that surround me. You say that nothing I will see – humpback whales, seals, penguins or polar bears – will compensate for not being able to feel and touch the textures and colours of this land. Well, maybe you are right. It may be quite depressing to be surrounded by ice and water. But it's only for three months. It's not forever. I can always stay in my cabin and listen to music or read, or even knit my coloured blanket that I still haven't finished.

Concentrate on the good things. Tell your friends and mine whatever crazy stories you can dream up. Tell them how your mother in her vintage years has fallen in love with a gorgeous man who is taking her to the end of the earth. Tell them how happy I am and what fun I intend having. Tell them I am glad to be alive – they should leave their small and petty lives and come sail with me.

My grandchildren need to be told other things. Tell them I am doing a project on whales and seals and will bring them back photographs and information that they will never find on the Web or on their CD-ROMs. Tell them I will persuade Charlie to come to their schools and talk to them about his adventures all over the world, and especially under the seas. He will capture their imaginations with his experiences of the world of dolphins and whales, and explain why he loves being in the water with the great white sharks. Tell them I will bring them gifts of rocks from glaciers, and examples of unusual Alaskan crafts, and I will tell them true stories of the Eskimos. Tell them I am going for their sake as well as mine. I want to share my experiences, especially with them.

Wish me luck, my children. I will be in touch wherever and whenever I can. After my travels, we can resume our e-mail correspondence with a new understanding of each other, and perhaps my other dream, that of elevating e-mail into a literary genre, will also be fulfilled one day.

I will always be there for you.

Much love
Mom